Bar Code →

P9-DGG-535

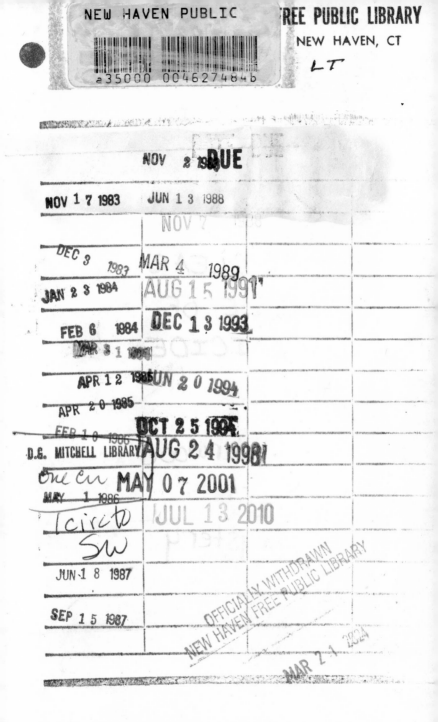

Laurence Deegan Q.C. had just won his latest case. At fifty, already a distinguished and famous barrister, he seemed set to become a judge at an early age.

The clerk in his Chambers notes something strange in Deegan's manner that same evening, the triumph still fresh. A few hours later Deegan ran the bath installed in his Chambers, got into it, and slit the veins in both wrists.

Why had he done it? His younger son (a police officer in the Special Branch) takes it upon himself to find out. It is this investigation that provides the core and the detail of a most intriguing mystery.

To all appearances Deegan's life was not merely beyond reproach, it was successful, happy, alive with hope and ambition. But there is no one who does not have a skeleton, major or minor, hidden somewhere. As Richard Deegan probed deeper he came across some baffling and contradictory evidence of episodes that his father had chosen to hide completely.

This story is most expertly constructed. Since there was no doubt that Deegan *had* killed himself there must – short of a brainstorm – have been a reason. The search to discover the reason makes this book gripping from first page to last, a fine example of Michael Underwood's subtle craftsmanship.

by the same author

"A CLEAR CASE OF SUICIDE"

Michael Underwood

FIC
C.2
MP

ST. MARTIN'S PRESS, NEW YORK

Library of Congress Cataloging in Publication Data

Underwood, Michael, 1916–
    A clear case of suicide.

    I.   Title.
PZ4.E94Cl   1980   [PR6055.V3]   823'.9'14   79-25389
ISBN 0-312-14326-5

For Parthenope

CHAPTER I

Almost before Laurence Deegan had left the Old Bailey, newspaper vans carrying the result of the case in their latest edition were hurtling to their delivery points around the metropolis.

'Financier Freed' and 'City Millionaire Toasts Justice in Champagne' were two of the headlines devised to titillate the exhausted commuter on his journey home.

The previous evening a paper had carried an item about Deegan himself, informing its readers that, though only fifty, he had been a Queen's Counsel for eight years and was widely tipped for early appointment as a High Court judge. The piece in question contained a number of inaccurate details about his life, speculated wildly about his earnings at the Bar and, to his considerable embarrassment, served the whole gossipy mixture up under the heading 'Silk In Fashion' – a reference to the silk gowns worn by Queen's Counsel.

Deegan eschewed self-advertisement as conscientiously as most of his professional brethren and had a genuine dislike of personal publicity. But the fact remained that he had recently had a run of forensic successes in cases which had attracted the public's attention and there was little he could do to prevent the sort of piece that had appeared. His clerk, Stanley, and his whole family were under a strict injunction not to answer reporters' questions, but, of course, if some journalist was minded to write something of that nature, a paucity of fact was seldom a deterrent.

'That result won't have done us any harm,' Stanley said complacently as he gathered up Deegan's belongings like a well-trained nanny. His robes, his brief, notebooks and several volumes of law reports were neatly assembled for taking back to Chambers.

'I imagine not. Though I'm never happy about getting someone off on a technicality.'

'It was one nobody else had spotted. Not even the judge. The prosecution went away with their tails right between their legs.' In the same self-satisfied tone, Stanley went on, 'I'm glad the judge paid you that compliment. He's not given to praise, so it was doubly acceptable.'

Deegan gave his clerk a tolerant smile. He knew Stanley was thinking in terms of the increased fees he would be demanding on his behalf in future, a percentage of which would go into Stanley's own pocket. Small wonder that the senior clerk in a busy set of Chambers could find himself earning considerably more than some of the junior barristers for whom he clerked.

Stanley had been the tea-boy when Deegan was first called to the Bar and became a member of Chambers in Mulberry Court. They had grown up together in the law and now Laurence Deegan was head of Chambers and Stanley one of the doyens of Temple clerks.

'I've fixed a consultation in that Official Secrets Act case. The solicitors were on the phone just before I left Chambers to come to court.'

'Oh, lord, I've not even opened the brief yet.'

'The consultation's not until the day after tomorrow.'

Deegan gave his clerk a wry glance. 'I suppose I shall have to read it this evening. I was going home to an empty flat anyway. My wife won't be home until nine, so I might as well stay in Chambers and work.'

Stanley nodded. 'Yes, the security people were anxious you shouldn't carry the brief around as it contains classified information. I've locked it in your wall safe.'

'I don't suppose it contains anything that a persevering spy couldn't discover without breaking the law. The trouble is that secrecy becomes an end in itself in these O.S.A. cases. The powers that be become paranoid on the subject.'

They had almost reached Chambers when Stanley said, 'You'll find a new brief from Chalmers & Co. on your desk. It arrived at lunchtime. There's a bit of urgency about that one too, I'm afraid.' Deegan frowned but his clerk didn't notice and went on, 'Perhaps you'd glance at it and then I'll phone Mr Chalmers tomorrow and fix a consultation.'

'I suppose you've already promised to do that.'

'I told him we'd do our best.'

It struck Deegan in his less benign moments that his clerk was overfond of the royal 'we', seeing that he was never the one who actually had to do the work. Fortunately, however, he had the right constitution for a busy silk's practice and relished all his success to the full. He had his sights set on a judgeship in due course, though not as imminently as the writer of the gossip item had speculated. He thought fifty-four or fifty-five would be about the right age to be appointed. So Fay, his wife, would just have to wait a few more years before becoming Lady Deegan.

'He wants you to undertake the defence of Terence Edward-Jones,' Stanley went on blithely. 'He's the young man charged with the murder of his girl-friend. You've probably seen his name in the papers. He's the son of Tom Edward-Jones, the property tycoon.'

'I've had my fill of millionaires,' Deegan said in a suddenly acerbic tone.

'Mr Chalmers was very anxious that you should take the brief. It's a paid defence and he suggested a brief fee of five thousand, with refreshers to match.' When Deegan didn't respond, the clerk went on in a hopeful voice, 'I gather it's by no means an open and shut case and the young man has quite a good run. Mr Chalmers already has a couple of medical experts lined up who'll say that the girl had a heart condition which would have inclined her to sudden death in certain circumstances. It sounds like our old friend vagal inhibition. You only have to half-prove that and a jury will reduce murder to manslaughter at the very least. Anyway, if you could take a look at the brief this evening, I'll call Mr Chalmers in the morning.'

They had arrived back at Chambers and, to Stanley's mild surprise, Deegan stalked ahead to his room at the end of the corridor without a further word. Normally, he would have poked his head round the door of the clerks' room and exchanged a greeting with whoever was there. There were invariably one or two members of Chambers sorting out their next day's work with John and Mark, Stanley's two young assistants.

Stanley stared at the retreating back with a puzzled expression. Something seemed to have suddenly upset his head of Chambers, but he had no idea what. His once variable moods had been less apparent in recent times. Indeed, ever since he had taken silk (that often unpredictable step for a barrister) and had abandoned much of the drudge work which had come to him as a member of the junior Bar. For him, becoming a Queen's Counsel had held fewer risks than for many and his practice had developed and expanded without a hiccup. Now, eight years after that event he had the legal world at his feet and was probably the most sought-after silk in general practice. Playing his part as a good clerk, Stanley had been careful to secure him as much civil as criminal work in order to broaden his experience and equip him for the judgeship which would certainly come his way. Not that Stanley had any wish to hasten that day, for Laurence Deegan's departure from Chambers would affect his pocket more than anyone's. It had been the same when Sam Hensley, an ex-head of Chambers, had been elevated to the Bench. But Stanley had learnt to be philosophical about such departures, reflecting that, even if the sea didn't exactly contain better fish than ever came out of it, there were still promising ones swimming around in the middle and upper reaches of Chambers.

Meanwhile, he had better try to find out what the trouble was with Deegan. There was doubtless something he could do to help. After all, the role of a barrister's clerk embraced everything from business manager to friend and nursemaid.

He knocked on the door and went in without waiting for an answer. Deegan was standing with his back to the door, staring out of the window. It was a familiar stance and the view across to the river was one that could never grow stale. But on this occasion there was something about the hunch of Deegan's shoulders that told Stanley he wasn't just admiring the view.

'Is every thing all right, Mr Deegan?' he asked in a faintly worried tone.

For several seconds there was no reply, then in a brittle voice Deegan said, 'I've been thinking, Stanley. I don't want to do that Official Secrets case.'

'But, Mr Deegan . . .' Stanley said in a shocked tone. 'What can I tell the instructing solicitor? The consultation's fixed . . . I mean . . .'

'I'm sure you'll be able to cope. After all, you spend your life making excuses for us and smoothing our paths. Nobody's better at it.'

'But you've not even read the brief yet. You said so on our way back from the Bailey.' He paused, but when Deegan went on gazing out of the window, continued in a tone that bore a note of umbrage, 'May I ask the reason for your sudden decision, sir? I think I'm entitled to know.'

'I don't care for those cases. I hate all the mumbo-jumbo and secrecy and parts of the trial being held in camera . . . I find the whole set-up distasteful.'

Stanley stared in disbelief at the silhouetted figure in the window. He thought his ears must be deceiving him. Deegan had never returned a brief once it had been delivered save when he had an unavoidable clash of fixtures. But in the Kulka case the date of trial had not even been settled. It would be Stanley's task to try to negotiate a date convenient to everyone.

When at length he found his tongue he said, 'If you really insist, of course I'll return the brief, but I don't know what I'm going to tell the solicitor. You're putting me in a most embarrassing situation, Mr Deegan. And you of all people who have the reputation of never letting anyone down! Have you said your last word?' Stanley waited but the figure at the window remained silent. 'May I make just one request? That you sleep on your decision and we talk about it again tomorrow.' Stanley turned to go when his eyes alighted on the wall safe. He walked over and, unlocking it, removed the brief which had rested there unopened for two weeks while Laurence Deegan's attention had been occupied with more immediate matters. Often briefs had to wait considerably longer than that before he could read them.

Returning to the desk he placed it in a prominent position next to the equally bulky set of papers that had arrived in the case of the Queen against Terence Edward-Jones.

'I've put the brief on your table,' he said reproachfully. 'You've never not listened to me before, so I'm asking you again to read it before you go home this evening. If you're still of the same mind

11

tomorrow, I won't argue further but will endeavour to extricate us from what will undoubtedly be a very awkward situation.'

As he turned to go, Laurence Deegan stepped back from the window and faced his clerk for the first time since he had entered the room. His expression was calm, but he had a strangely detached air.

'Don't think too harshly of me, Stanley. Just accept that I have my reasons.' He gave his clerk a wistful smile. 'I don't want to talk about it any further, but if I did, you would be the person I'd consult. I'll certainly do as you request and read the brief.' He glanced at his watch. 'You might let it be known that I don't wish to be disturbed. Before you leave, put an outside line through to my extension. I'll lock up when I go.'

He stepped over to his desk and stared down at the brief his clerk had placed there. For several seconds, Stanley hovered with his hand resting on the door knob. He appeared racked by indecision, wanting to speak but not knowing what to say. Seldom short of words, he found himself mentally tongue-tied.

Finally, in an unnaturally stiff tone he said, 'I'll wish you good night, sir.' But he received no reply.

By seven o'clock everyone had left, the last conference having broken up a few minutes earlier.

'Sorry if I've kept you, Stanley,' Alan Crombie said, standing in the doorway of the clerks' room. He was dressed for departure and was carrying a brief-case. 'I'm afraid my con went on longer than I expected.'

'You're not the last. Mr Deegan's still here.'

'Oh, I'll go and poke my head round his door and say hello. I've not seen him for several days.'

'Better not, Mr Crombie. He particularly said he didn't wish to be disturbed.'

Alan Crombie raised a surprised eyebrow, but Stanley declined to meet his gaze.

'I'll say good night then, Stanley. I'm at Cambridge Crown Court tomorrow, so you won't see me.'

'Phone in at the end of the day and let me know the state of play, sir.'

'But of course, Stanley. When have I ever not?'

'I know you're better than most. I almost need to send out

search parties for one or two members of Chambers when they're out of London.'

'Not guilty! In any event my case won't last long. It's a plea. But I'll phone to find out where I am the next day.'

For several seconds after Alan Crombie's departure, Stanley stared across the room. Should he make one final attempt to find out the reason for Laurence Deegan's unusual behaviour? Almost two hours had passed since he had left him alone in his room. Two hours during which he might have been on the other side of the moon for the silence that had reigned. And now they were the only two people left in Chambers. Might it not be the moment to go and broach him again? But somehow he shrank from the prospect, a hitherto undreamt of possibility in their relationship.

He rose from his desk and went out into the passage. He could see a light shining beneath Deegan's door and began to walk slowly toward it. For a couple of seconds, he stood poised to knock, but then he returned forlornly to his own room.

Picking up a phone, he buzzed Deegan's extension.

'Yes?'

'I'm just going, Mr Deegan. Thought I'd better let you know.'

'Thank you, Stanley. Good night.'

'Anything else before I go?'

'Nothing,' Deegan said and rang off. It was as if he sensed his clerk's inclination to prolong the conversation and decided to give him no opportunity.

Stanley had seldom felt so ill at ease as he left Chambers and made his way home. He hoped that everything might be seen differently in the morning and that the evening's events would assume the proportions of a bad dream, which had passed with the new day. But deep down he realised he was hoping for a miracle.

It was as if the head of Chambers had undergone some sudden mental transformation. One minute he had been on top of the world, the next he had been mysteriously stricken.

There had to be an explanation. But what was it?

CHAPTER II

Fay Deegan was surprised to find the flat in darkness when she arrived home shortly after nine o'clock. She wasn't so much worried as faintly cross that her husband wasn't there to welcome her with a drink. He had known she was going down to Bristol to visit her sister who was in hospital after a serious operation and he might have guessed that she would arrive back tired after a trying day.

They lived in an expensive flat, a stone's throw from Kensington High Street, into which they had moved after the boys had grown up and left home. Norris, their elder son, was now twenty-five and had recently been called to the Bar. He and his wife, Joanna, lived in a tiny flat in the Paddington area. He was not in his father's Chambers which was a relief to both of them. Against his parents' wishes he had married before he qualified, though their unspoken objection had been to Joanna herself whom neither of them liked.

Richard, their younger son, had been adopted when he was a baby, after Fay had been told she would never be able to have any further children of her own. He was two years younger than Norris and had proved to be not only a much more affectionate son than his brother, but generally easier in every way. He had more than repaid his adoptive parents for everything they had done for him. The contrast in behaviour of the two boys was something they still found painful to dwell on.

As soon as he had left school at the age of eighteen, Richard fulfilled an ambition and joined the Metropolitan Police. He was now a detective constable in the Special Branch at Scotland

Yard and lived in official accommodation. He had a girl-friend called Sophie whom his parents liked considerably better than their daughter-in-law.

Fay picked up a letter from the mat inside the front door. It was a bill and she tossed it on to the hall table. Obviously her husband hadn't come in and gone out again or the letter wouldn't have still been on the mat. She wondered whether he would want anything to eat when he returned. She had had a sandwich on the train and was not hungry. Her appetite was little larger than a sparrow's anyway, her husband was always asserting.

She rarely took a drink alone and as he was not there to pour her one, she decided to make herself a cup of tea instead.

Having turned on lights and drawn curtains, she wandered into the living-room with her tea. She had been home twenty minutes and there had been no calls. She had told Laurence which train she would be catching, so he must know she would be back by now.

If he was not going to call her, she had better call him. He was presumably working away in Chambers, totally unaware of the time. She would remind him.

But his telephone rang without answer. She knew that when he stayed late in Chambers, he had his extension connected to the direct line. Either Stanley had forgotten or Laurence was already on his way home. It was also just possible that he had gone to dine on the Bench of his Inn. To his intense pleasure, he had recently been elected a Bencher, which meant eating at the high table in the company of judges and other leading members of the profession.

She had barely sat down when her own phone began to ring. That will be him now, she thought, as she walked across to answer it.

'Mum? I thought I'd call to see if you'd got back safely. Also to find out how Aunt Ruth is.'

'Oh, it's you, Richard! I thought it must be your father. I got home about half an hour ago. I found Ruth reasonably cheerful and one of the nurses said they were pleased with her progress. But oh, how I hate hospital visiting! I always feel it's I who've been through the mangle, not the unfortunate patients.'

'I suspect most healthy people feel that way,' he said with a laugh. 'I remember when you used to visit me after I'd had my appendix removed, I always felt you were much more in need of the grapes and Lucozade than I was. Mind you, I don't think Dad was much better, but he'd had more practice at hiding his feelings. You can't get on at the Bar without the ability to simulate. How is Dad, by the way?'

'He isn't in yet.'

'Probably working late in Chambers.'

'I've just tried to call him there, but couldn't get any reply.'

'He must be on his way home then. By the way, all right to come to supper on Saturday?'

'Of course.'

'And bring Sophie?'

'Naturally.'

'Fine.'

'You've not said anything about yourself, Richard. Is everything going all right?'

'I'd tell you soon enough if it wasn't. But it happens to be great at the moment.'

'Well, do take care! You're in a dangerous job dealing with dangerous people.'

Richard gave a cheerful laugh. 'Everyone's job is dangerous these days, Mum. Mine's no more so than many. One can't live wrapped in cotton wool.'

'That's the last thing I'd want you to do,' she said defensively.

'I know, Mum, I was only joking.'

'Just don't let familiarity breed contempt.'

'If only the public really knew. Most Special Branch work is utterly hum-drum. Trouble is everyone thinks we spend our time hunting spies and infiltrating terrorist cells.'

'Don't you do that, too?'

'Only on red letter days. Seriously, Mum, don't worry about me!'

Fay Deegan realised there was no profit in pursuing the topic. She knew that what he said about his job was true and, moreover, she wasn't really the worrying sort.

'Have you seen Norris recently?' she enquired.

'No. Why?'

'I just wondered. We don't see much of him either.'

'Joanna makes it rather obvious that she doesn't like Sophie,' Richard remarked. 'But I talk to Norris on the telephone from time to time. Nothing wrong with them, is there?'

'No, but I like to think you keep in touch with your brother. It's easier for you than for us in some ways. If Joanna could have her way, we'd never meet again save on formal family occasions. She's always regarded me as a competitor for Norris' affections, which is absurd.'

'At least you like Sophie and she likes you.'

'She's a sweet girl.' Fay was sensible enough not to add that, nevertheless, she didn't really regard her as quite good enough for her son.

'I must ring off, Mum. Love to Dad when he comes in and see you on Saturday. About seven o'clock.'

Fay reckoned that her husband must be home within the next ten minutes. He always drove to Chambers and was one of the lucky ones with a permit to park in the Temple. At this hour of the evening when the rush hour was over, he could make the journey comfortably in twelve to fifteen minutes.

At ten o'clock when he had still not returned, she decided to ring Chambers again. It was just possible that she had misdialled the first time and got connected to the number of someone who wasn't there to answer and point out her mistake.

On this occasion, she dialled with extra care and let the number ring two dozen times before giving up.

Where on earth could he be? And why hadn't he called her? It was most unlike him not to do so. Many husbands were more than casual about letting their wives know when they were held up and going to be late, but not Laurence. He was most meticulous and if he couldn't call himself, he would get Stanley or one of the junior clerks to do so.

She had hardly sat down when she jumped up again. That was it, she would phone Stanley. He would be aware of her husband's plans for the evening.

She reached for her handbag in which she kept her address book. It was ridiculous, but she always had difficulty recalling his surname. For twenty-five years he had been just Stanley. She was sure, however, that his last name began with one of the earlier letters of the alphabet. Yes, here it was: Stanley Beresford,

17

099 3006. She dialled the number and a few seconds later heard Stanley's voice on the line.

'This is Fay Deegan, Stanley. I'm sorry to bother you at home, but I wonder if you know what my husband was doing this evening?' She gave a small, brittle laugh. 'I was expecting to find him here when I got back an hour ago, but he hasn't come in and he hasn't called me.'

'He was staying in Chambers to work, Mrs Deegan. He must still be there.'

'I've phoned a couple of times and got no answer. He does have an outside line put through to his room, doesn't he?'

'Yes. It was the last thing I did before I left. Would you like me to try and get through to him and call you back?'

'Will you do that? I would be grateful. He'll probably walk through the door as soon as I ring off,' she added with another short laugh.

But he didn't, nor did Stanley have any more luck in raising a response.

It was not more than three minutes before he called back.

'Is he home yet, Mrs Deegan?' he asked as soon as Fay answered.

'No. I take it you couldn't get any reply either?'

'No.'

Fay found that her mouth had gone suddenly dry. There was something in Stanley's tone which had sparked off a feeling of panic.

'Did he seem all right when you left Chambers?' she asked in a voice she scarcely recognised as her own.

She thought Stanley wasn't going to answer, but then he said in a careful tone, 'He did seem unusually preoccupied.'

'What about?'

'I don't know. He seemed to be worried about one of his cases.'

'Was that all?' she said with a note of relief.

'Yes.'

'Did he mention that I was going to be late home?'

'Yes. When I told him there were two briefs requiring rather urgent attention, he said he might as well work late in Chambers as you wouldn't be home until nine o'clock. Incidentally, he had a great triumph at the Old Bailey this afternoon.'

'I read the result in a paper on the train.' She paused. 'What do you think we'd better do, Stanley?'

'I'll go up to Chambers immediately and see if I can find out what's happened.'

'That is good of you. It'll certainly set my mind at rest. How long will it take you to get there?'

'I'll get my son to run me to the Temple in his car. It won't take more than fifteen minutes at this hour. I'll call you as soon as I arrive.'

'I'll be waiting beside the telephone.'

She now felt sure that her husband must have had a heart attack and was lying dead on the floor of his room. What other explanation could there be? He had never shown any signs of heart trouble and was moderate in all his habits, but such were the pressures of work on him that the possibility of being struck down by a coronary must be ever present. Men younger than he had been stricken before now.

She tried to distract herself by performing minor domestic chores, but finally gave up and sat down with the telephone within reach. Glancing at her watch, she tried to visualise Stanley's progress toward the Temple. Half an hour ago she had not been unduly worried, but now panic was seeping through her whole body like floodwater bubbling up relentlessly between floorboards.

Leaving his son waiting in the car, Stanley ran up the two flights of stairs to Chambers.

The main door was fitted with an allegedly burglar-proof mortice lock, as well as with a normal Yale lock. When he had departed shortly after seven o'clock that evening, he had merely released the catch on the Yale lock.

Nevertheless he now inserted his key into the mortice lock. If it could be unlocked, that would surely mean Laurence Deegan must have left Chambers; though he didn't pause to consider why that should be any cause for reassurance. But he quickly realised that the tongue of the lock was still in a retracted position and inserting his other key, he opened the door and stepped inside.

19

The light shining beneath the door of Deegan's room was unmistakable in the otherwise dark interior of Chambers.

He, too, was now certain that head of Chambers had been taken seriously ill, if not worse than that. He bounded down the passage and flung open the door.

The room was empty.

He stood staring about him, taking in the scene like a photographer indiscriminately clicking his camera at everything in sight. He noticed the two briefs still lying on the desk. Each was neatly tied and showed no sign of having been opened, though Stanley could tell they weren't in the same position he had placed them.

With a sudden exclamation, he sprang forward. If Deegan had collapsed and fallen out of his chair, his body could be on the floor hidden from view by the desk.

But a second later he was satisfied that the head of Chambers was nowhere in his room. Nor could he find any written note indicating where he had gone.

He hurried to the clerks' room to see if any message had been left on his own desk. But once again he drew blank.

He was about to call Fay when a small sound came to his ears. It was quite faint and at first he couldn't make out what it was. Then he realised it was the gentle gurgle of water and came from the bathroom with which Chambers had been endowed when reconstructed after the war. It was used mostly by senior members who didn't have time to go home before an evening engagement.

His heart missed a beat when he tried the door and found it locked. He banged on it heavily.

'Are you in there, Mr Deegan? Can you hear me?'

But the only sound was the continuing mild gurgle of water lapping the overflow pipe. He thought he could also detect the quiet flow of water from a tap.

Dashing downstairs, he shouted to his son who was still in the car.

'I'm afraid something awful has happened, Brian. We'll have to break open the bathroom door,' he said breathlessly as his son joined him. Together they raced back upstairs.

'Got an axe or a crowbar?' Brian Beresford enquired after testing the strength of the door.

'There's an axe on the landing above. It's part of the fire-fighting equipment.'

Brian gave a grunt and shot away. A few seconds later, he returned carrying it in a purposeful manner.

'Stand back, Dad,' he said as he prepared to swing it at the lock.

There was a sharp splintering of wood, but it required two further blows before the lock yielded and the door flew open. Each let out an involuntary cry of horror at the scene inside. Laurence Deegan lay in a bath brimming with pink water. The hot tap was running gently and the water gurgled lazily down the overflow pipe.

His head was resting against the back of the bath, but lolled to the left as if he had dropped off to sleep. His eyes were shut and his skin the colour of watered milk. On the ledge at the further side of the bath lay an open razor, its blade extended.

'Come on, Dad, nothing we can do for him. Better go and phone the police,' Brian said, as his father stood staring in numbed horror.

'He might still be alive,' Stanley said in a painful whisper.

Brian went across and placed a hand on Deegan's forehead. Then bending further over the bath, he lifted his left hand out of the water and turned it to expose the wrist. There were two superficial cuts and a much deeper and more deadly one that had severed the artery. He reached across to examine the other wrist. This bore a single deep slash.

'He's dead all right. I'll turn off the tap,' he said in a practical voice. He was a hospital laboratory technician who had ceased to be squeamish at gruesome sights. As he straightened up, the telephone in Deegan's room began to ring.

'That'll be Mrs Deegan,' Stanley said with an effort.

'Better go and answer it, Dad,' Brian said when his father showed no sign of moving. 'You'll have to break it to her some-time.'

It seemed at first as if Stanley was unable to wrench his gaze away from the piece of Grand Guignol in the bathroom, but eventually he turned and disappeared down the passage.

21

When he returned, Brian had half-closed the bathroom door and was standing outside.

'Was it Mrs Deegan?'

'Yes. She wanted to come immediately, but I persuaded her not to. She's going to call her sons.' Stanley glanced toward the bathroom with tears starting to fall down his cheeks. 'Poor man, what on earth made him do it? He had everything going his way...'

Brian gave his father a concerned look. He could understand what an appalling shock it had been to him. For the past few years, Laurence Deegan's career had dominated his working life. Everything revolved about him and his name was never long absent from conversation. Stanley was not only proud of his own contribution to a prospering career, but proud, too, of the personal relationship which grows up between a barrister and his clerk and which someone had once likened to that between a shepherd and his dog.

Brian moved toward the door of the clerks' room. In a brisk tone, he said, 'Time to call the police, Dad.'

CHAPTER III

The police, who came within fifteen minutes, were efficient and polite.

Brian had found some brandy while they awaited their arrival and had poured his father a large measure. He introduced himself to the uniformed inspector and explained what had happened, while Stanley sat looking dazed in his chair.

'That the bathroom?' the inspector enquired, glancing at the splintered door. Followed by a young constable and Brian, he walked across and pushed it open. 'No question about his intention!' he remarked after a cursory examination of the body in the bath. 'I've sometimes wondered which method I'd choose if I was going to end my life. I know one thing: it wouldn't be this. Whose razor is it? Mr Deegan's?'

'I'll ask my father.'

'Don't worry. We can ask him in a minute. Wonder why he did it? Found a note of any sort? They usually leave one.'

'That's something else you'll have to ask my father.'

The inspector nodded thoughtfully. 'He was a good after-dinner speaker, Mr Deegan. Came to one of our police functions a few months ago. Very entertaining he was. Told a number of funny stories about judges which went down well. Everyone said he was bound to be one himself soon. A judge, I mean.' He shook himself as if suddenly aware it wasn't the occasion for social reminiscence. 'We'd better get a doctor along, just to estimate time of death. After that the body can be removed to the mortuary. There'll have to be a post mortem and the coroner will need to be informed.' He frowned slightly and peered at

23

Brian. 'I suppose none of this really affects you. You're only here by chance, so to speak, though I'm afraid that won't save you from giving us a statement and probably being called as a witness at the inquest. Anyway, let's go and have a word with your father.'

Stanley seemed to have emerged from his initial shock when they returned to the clerks' room.

'I've been explaining to your son what the next steps are, Mr Beresford,' the inspector said in a friendly tone. 'But I expect you know them as well as I do. Did Mr Deegan leave a note?'

Stanley shook his head. 'I looked for one before I knew what had actually happened. I merely thought he wasn't here and might have left a note explaining where he'd gone.'

'Don't mind if I take a look around in a moment?'

'Of course not.'

'By the way, whose razor is that in the bathroom?'

Stanley gave a small shudder. 'Mr Hallick's. He's the oldest member of Chambers.'

'I noticed his name on the door outside.'

George Hallick was now well into his seventies, though his exact age was known only to himself. He always wore a wing collar and an old-fashioned black jacket with ancient pin-stripe trousers. It was an outfit of which he seemed to possess an inexhaustible supply, all the items appearing to be of the same antiquity.

'Mr Hallick uses the bathroom here as it saves his fuel bill at home,' Stanley went on with a faint wisp of a smile. 'The razor's been there as long as I recall.'

'Where was it normally kept?'

'In the cupboard above the wash basin.'

Stanley didn't add that it was almost the only item which was now kept there. Other members of Chambers had ceased to leave their toothpaste and after-shave when they discovered that George Hallick used them as if they were on free issue.

The inspector sighed. 'I gather you've informed his widow?'

'Yes.'

'That's something I've never got used to, breaking bad news to people. Not even after all these years.' He shook his head lugubriously, then in a brisker tone said, 'While we're waiting for the doctor, I'll take a quick look round. Perhaps you'd show me Mr Deegan's room.'

It was another hour and a half before Stanley and his son were able to lock up and depart. The doctor had not spent more than five minutes at the scene. He was a taciturn man at the best of times and never more so than when called out at night. After he had gone, Laurence Deegan's body had been lifted from the bath and carried out on a stretcher to the waiting ambulance. Fortunately, the 'Temple being an oasis of quiet at that hour of night, there had been only a stray cat to observe his departure. Finally, after a sample of the bath water had been taken, ('Just in case somebody wants to analyse it, though I can't see why they should,' the inspector had said) the plug had been pulled out and the remainder allowed to drain away.

But there was still one thing Stanley felt compelled to do before leaving.

'I must give the bath a good clean, Brian. I couldn't bear to come in tomorrow and see it all smeared with blood the way it is now. It's going to be bad enough without that.'

CHAPTER IV

Laurence Deegan's death stunned everyone in the legal world. Tributes were paid and Fay received over a hundred letters of condolence.

His immediate colleagues in Mulberry Court were the most shocked of all. To lose their head of Chambers in such a manner was unnerving. It was, nevertheless, remarkable that not one of them affected to be wise after the event. Not a single voice was raised to suggest that the speaker had always suspected he might end his own life.

George Hallick hardly endeared himself by button-holing any-one within reach and asserting how unfair of Deegan it had been to use his razor for the deed. He obviously regarded it as a personal affront. Eventually he was told that everyone had heard enough and that his reaction was in poor taste. This, however, did nothing to alter his conviction that it had been most un-reasonable of head of Chambers to select that particular instru-ment with which to kill himself.

The coroner, to whom the event was reported, was quickly satisfied that it was a clear case of suicide and consequently released the body for burial before holding an inquest. The pathologist's findings were that the deceased man had bled to death following the severing of arteries in each wrist. He had added in his report that it was a classic method of suicide, being particularly associated with lying in a bath of water.

The funeral which took place a week later was private at Fay's request. Stanley attended, accompanied by two or three members of Chambers, as did Mr Justice Hensley, a fellow Bencher of his Inn and a previous head of Chambers.

Fay had felt unequal to facing a large funeral attended by representatives of all the organisations her husband had been associated with. They would have their opportunity later when a memorial service was held. At least, she had assumed one would be held until Norris hinted that the authorities might consider it improper in the case of someone who had taken his own life.

As she stood at the door of the church after the service with Norris and Richard on either side, she suddenly realised that the coming weeks were going to be much worse than the one that had passed since his death. The aftermath of tragedy is always the hardest part when one is left to pick up the broken pieces of one's life.

Richard, of course, had been a great strength to her and Norris, too, in his own way. If only he wasn't so cool and detached, like a disdainful *maître d'*. Joanna, his wife, had gone through all the right motions and said all the correct things, but they came out as if she had put them on tape and merely had to press a button to produce them.

Fay could not help noticing how Joanna was now standing with her back half-turned on Richard's Sophie so as not to have to talk to her.

'Here comes Mr Justice Hensley. Mother,' Norris whispered to her in a strained voice.

'It was kind of you to come, Sam,' she said, holding out her hand.

'What can I say to you, Fay?' He glanced at her sons. 'I'm only thankful that you have Norris and Richard to support you in your bereavement. You must let me know if there's anything I can do. As you must be aware, the whole profession has been shocked by Laurence's death.'

'But why did he do it, Sam?' she said in a voice that trembled.

The judge shook his head in incomprehension and gave her hand a squeeze before passing on.

The interment was to be attended by family only, so that the remainder of the congregation now made for their cars.

Leaving his mother's side, Richard suddenly darted after Stanley and caught him as he was about to get into a car.

'May I come and see you some time?' he asked, slightly out of breath.

'Of course. Very happy to see you any time.'

'What about this evening?'

'I take it you want to have a bit of a chat?'

'Yes.'

'Then let's say six o'clock. Things have quietened down by that hour.'

Stanley had always liked Richard. He had a shrewd notion why he wished to come and see him and welcomed the prospect of a heart to heart talk with a member of Laurence Deegan's family. His only contact until today had been when Norris had called round and said in a faintly militant tone that he would like to make an inventory of his father's law books.

When Richard arrived at Chambers that evening, he found Mark in charge of the clerks' room. He was operating the small switchboard and raised a helpless eyebrow at Richard.

'Are you Mr Deegan?' he asked when eventually free to speak. 'Stanley's expecting you. He's just having a word with Mr Crombie.'

Though Richard hadn't reached an age when he could be made to feel old, the new junior clerk in his father's Chambers almost managed to achieve that effect. He couldn't be more than eighteen.

'We've not met,' he said, advancing into the small room and holding out his hand.

'I've only been here a couple of months.'

'Liking it?'

'Ye-es.'

'You sound a bit doubtful.'

'Not really. It's just that it's unlike anything one could ever have imagined.'

'How did you come to the job?'

'A friend of my father knows Stanley. I'd always said I didn't want an ordinary office job and I'd turned down every suggestion anyone made and my parents were getting a bit fed up. I'd no idea what being a barrister's clerk involved, but it sounded

28

ifferent.' He grinned. 'It's that all right. The Temple must be
ne of the few citadels of uninhibited free enterprise left in the
ountry.'

'And that appeals to you?'

'I'm ready to give it a whirl,' he said with another grin. 'Especi-
lly now I've seen the sort of money that can be earned if you
tay the course and are in the right Chambers.' His expression
:louded over. 'Incidentally, terrible thing about your father. I
neant to say that before.'

'Thanks. Did you know him at all?'

'Only as a figure who came and went. Stanley always looked
ιfter him personally. But he was very nice to me on the few
)ccasions we met. Knew my name from the start and that sort
)f thing. My first big moment came when I had to take a cup
)f tea along to his room on my second day here and he asked
ne some friendly questions about myself. You're in the police,
ιren't you?'

'Yes.'

'That was one of the outfits I thought of joining, but then I
decided I wouldn't like working shift hours. Aren't you in the
Special Branch?'

'Yes, but I still have to work shifts at times. It's not as
glamorous as most people believe.'

'But it's better than pounding a beat?'

'Sure, though I did my stint of that when I first joined.'

'One thing about this job, you meet all sorts and kinds. It's
a good spot for keeping eyes and ears open. You married?'

'Not yet.'

Mark made a face. 'You won't catch me falling for that lark
yet awhile. You know John, the number two clerk? He's gone
off early this evening to buy an engagement ring.' His tone was
a blend of pity and astonishment at the gullibility of a fellow male.

'Some are cut out for early marriage,' Richard said, feeling
he had to stick up for the viewpoint.

Further discussion, however, was foreclosed by Stanley's
arrival in the room.

'Sorry to have kept you waiting, Richard. Shall we go along to
your father's old room? It's still unoccupied and we shan't be

disturbed.' He gave Mark a quick glance. 'Everything under control?'

For answer, Mark held up a confident thumb.

'He seems a bright kid,' Richard said as he followed Stanley along the passage.

'Of course, you wouldn't have met him before. Too early to know whether he'll be any good. His trouble will be learning to keep his brightness within proper limits. He tends to want to run before he can even crawl decently.'

Richard smiled at the tone of paternalistic reproof. As he stepped into his father's familiar room and Stanley closed the door behind him, he had a strange feeling. Nothing seemed to have been moved. It was as if the room was being preserved as a reminder of its recent occupant. He suddenly noticed, however, that the silver-framed photograph of his mother with Norris and himself when small boys had gone. It had always stood on the right of the desk. Now tactfully put away by Stanley no doubt.

'Let's sit down!' Stanley's voice broke in on his reverie.

Richard swallowed hard and pulled out a chair from the wall.

'Your father used to enjoy your occasional visits to Chambers,' Stanley went on as though reading Richard's mind. 'He was very proud of you. But of course you know that.'

'I used to be certain I was interrupting something terribly important when I came. Not that he gave that impression. But he always seemed to have so much work. I don't know how he survived.'

'It's a question of training. Those that can't cope with the pressures go off and do something else. If they're sufficiently senior they apply for a circuit judgeship. That's a breed that's multiplied in recent years like insects after a summer shower. The Lord Chancellor must sometimes wonder where he's going to find any more. But he does.' Stanley allowed himself a wintry smile. 'Of course there are some who'll never accept a circuit judgeship – not worth it financially – and others who'll go on beating hopefully on the door until their knuckles are bleeding. We've got a few of both in these Chambers, as your father may have told you. Of course, he was destined for the High Court Bench. And quite soon, too, if all the rumours were correct.' He paused and let out a sigh. 'But you haven't come to hear my views on the state of the profession.'

'You can probably guess why I'm here,' Richard said, nervously biting his lip.

'You're looking for clues as to why he took his life?'

'I'm determined to find out why,' he said vehemently. 'I was extremely fond of my father. He was a fine man who apparently had everything going his way, when suddenly out of the blue this happens. There has to be an explanation, Stanley. It wasn't as if he was subject to depressions. Moreover, the post mortem failed to disclose any natural disease. At first, I thought that might be the explanation. That he had sneaked off to see a specialist without telling anyone and had had some form of untreatable cancer diagnosed and had decided to end everything before he lost his grip. But there was nothing like that. He was as physically and mentally fit as any fifty-year-old can expect to be. So what made him do it, Stanley?'

It was several seconds before the clerk spoke.

'I suppose,' he said in a slow tone, 'that I've given that question as much thought as you have, Richard. The police have pressed me for some sort of answer for the coroner. People who commit suicide without leaving behind any word of explanation defeat the system so to speak.'

'You were the last person to see him, Stanley. You walked back from court with him that evening. Surely there must have been some sign on the horizon.'

'Oh, there was that all right. It came just after I'd told him that the solicitors in his Official Secrets Act case wanted an early consultation. The news didn't appear to perturb him at first. Indeed, he said that as your mother wouldn't be home until late, he would work on the brief in Chambers. Then while we were still walking back from the Old Bailey I mentioned another brief that had come in and needed his urgent attention. It was the defence in the case of Terence Edward-Jones who is charged with the murder of his girl-friend. His father's Tom Edward-Jones, the property tycoon. I remember at that point your father made some remark to the effect he was tired of millionaires. I thought he was joking, but suddenly realised that he wasn't. When we arrived back in Chambers he went straight to his room

31

without a further word of any sort, which wasn't like him at all. About twenty minutes later I thought I had better go and see him and make sure everything was all right – I was more puzzled than worried – and I found him standing at the window, staring out. He didn't look round when I came in and then he dropped this bombshell about not wanting to do the O.S. case. Said he wanted me to return the brief.'

'Didn't he give you any explanation?'

'He just said he found such cases obnoxious with all their secrecy aspects and refused to talk about it any further. He did agree to read the brief, but I felt sure he wasn't going to change his mind. It was as though an iron shutter had suddenly descended and cut me off from him. It wasn't until I was about to leave the room that he turned away from the window and looked at me. All he said was, "Don't think too harshly of me, Stanley. Just accept that I have my reasons." ' Stanley shook his head slowly in recollection. 'I never saw him again,' he said in a tight voice. 'Just before I left I rang through on his extension and asked if there was anything he wanted before I went and he merely said no and wished me good night.'

'How did he sound at that point?'

'Calm, but still as if there was this shutter between us.' Stanley paused. 'Of course, I've told all this to the police, Richard.'

'The police interest ends with the inquest. Mine doesn't. The verdict has to be suicide, there can't be any dispute about that. But I'm not going to rest until I've found out why he killed himself. I'm prepared to devote every spare minute I have to digging away for the explanation. From what you've told me, it seems a fair assumption that it lies buried somewhere in a brief.'

'I've thought of that, too, Richard, but it just isn't plausible. What on earth could there have been in a brief that caused him to do what he did? It simply isn't credible.'

'It depends, doesn't it?' Richard observed 'Anyway, it's an aspect I'm going to explore. I suppose there's no chance of my having an unofficial look at the two briefs you've told me about?' Seeing what he took to be Stanley's slightly outraged expression, he added quickly, 'After all I am a Special Branch officer and,

32

as such, have had various security clearances, so it'll be like the secrets of the confessional as far as I'm concerned.'

'It's not that, Richard, but they're not in Chambers any longer. I had to return them both.' A look of professional chagrin came over his face. 'I tried to persuade each of the solicitors to let me pass them to Mr Kiley who took silk last year and who is extremely capable, but they decided to take the briefs elsewhere and I could only comply with their wishes.'

'Is it possible for you to give me the names of the two firms of solicitors?'

'In the Edward-Jones case, it was Chalmers & Co. of Marylebone. The brief came from Mr Oliver Chalmers. It was the first time he'd used these Chambers, so it hasn't turned out a very propitious start to our relationship. The Official Secrets Act case came from Messrs Weinstock & Walper, whose offices are in West London.'

'Are they one of your regulars?'

'They send quite a lot of work to the middle reaches of Chambers, though it would have been the first time they instructed your father.'

'There was nothing special about the O.S. case, was there? I know a bit about it from being in Special Branch, but it sounded a fairly routine case of its sort. After all, Peter Kulka was only a minor clerk in the Ministry of Defence.'

'He'd worked for a time in the minister's private office. He'd also served in the Defence Attaché's section at our embassy in Prague.'

'Was that where he was supposed to have been suborned?'

'Yes.'

Richard was thoughtful for a while.

'And yet,' he said in a musing tone, 'my father wanted to return the brief before he'd even looked at it – and after it had been sitting around in his room for a couple of weeks. It doesn't make sense, does it? One would have expected him either to return it immediately, *or* after reading it and discovering some professional reason for not defending. But it wasn't either. Just a totally unreasonable and inexplicable rejection. Do you think it's possible he had looked at it earlier in the week without mentioning the fact?'

'He could have. But why, when I told him of the consultation I'd arranged, did he say he hadn't opened it yet?'

'He might have had some reason for not wanting to tell you.'

'It strikes me as most unlikely, but then . . .'

'What happened later was even more unlikely; is that what you were about to say?'

Stanley nodded. 'Yes,' he said in a dejected tone.

'I suppose most of the witnesses were ministry officials and officers from the security service?'

'As far as I know, yes.'

'Who was Kulka's contact on the other side?'

'Somebody in the Czech Embassy. He's been sent home.'

'I bet he has. They don't leave them hanging around once they've been blown.' Richard pursed his lips. 'I'll have an un-official word with Detective Superintendent Alcester who's in charge of the case at our end. He's a nice man and will, I'm sure, tell me anything he properly can.'

'I can't see what on earth he can tell you, Richard, that'll help solve the mystery of your father's death.'

'Frankly, nor can I. But I've got to start somewhere. Incident-ally, you mentioned that the solicitor in the other case hadn't previously sent work to these Chambers. Any idea why he sent my father that particular brief?'

'Apparently on the express instructions of the defendant's father who had said he wanted Mr Deegan and no one else to handle the defence. I can quote you almost verbatim the final paragraph of the instructions to counsel drawn by Mr Chalmers. They were sufficiently unusual to imprint themselves on my mind. They ran something like this. "The accused is the son of Mr Thomas Edward-Jones, an extremely wealthy and most forceful man who insisted personally that the brief should be delivered to Mr Deegan. Mr Edward-Jones wishes to meet counsel in early consultation concerning his son's defence. Counsel ought to be aware that Mr Edward-Jones senior is a most deter-mined character and is prepared to spare no effort in fighting for his son's acquittal." '

'And that brief arrived only hours before my father's death,' Richard murmured thoughtfully.

Stanley nodded. 'If you decide to visit Mr Chalmers, you may find him a bit on the starchy side. Not at all like Mr Weinstock.'

As Richard left Chambers, he felt that he had at least made a start on his quest. It might easily prove to be a false one. Indeed he was prepared to find himself embarking on a number of false trails.

But somewhere there had to be an explanation of his father's death and he was absolutely determined to uncover it.

CHAPTER V

As he was in the Temple, he thought he might as well see if Norris was in his Chambers, though he didn't really expect to find him still there – always assuming he had put in an appearance at all after the funeral. In any event, his was not yet the sort of practice that kept him working late. Moreover, Richard knew that he was inclined to take his work home rather than stay late in Chambers, mainly to appease Joanna who otherwise complained.

Nevertheless, as he was so close, he decided to make the visit on the offchance of finding his brother. He had just turned into the entrance when he came face to face with Norris at the foot of the staircase.

'What on earth are you doing here?' Norris asked in a startled voice.

'I've been to see Stanley and thought I'd call on you; not that I really expected to find you here.'

'What've you been seeing Stanley about?' Norris asked suspiciously.

'I wanted to find out if he had any notion why Dad killed himself.'

'And did he have?'

'No.'

It seemed that Norris relaxed slightly. 'The only explanation is that he had a sudden brainstorm,' he said.

'Do you really believe that?'

'What else is there to believe?'

'There has to be some better explanation.'

36

'I doubt whether we shall ever know it. Look, Richard, I can't stand here talking. I just dashed in to pick up a brief for tomorrow and I promised Joanna I'd go straight back. We have some friends coming to supper. You're going to Mother's this evening, aren't you?'

'Yes, Sophie and I are going.'

'She seems to be bearing up well. Mother, I mean.' He paused, then giving his brother a reproving frown he went on, 'Father's dead, Richard, and nothing can bring him back. It's not going to help if you spend your spare time raking over what's happened and trying to delve into the past. I know you're upset. We're all upset, but it's the present we've got to live in, not the past.'

'I'm determined to find out why Dad did it,' Richard said quietly.

Norris let out a theatrical sigh. 'Well, for Heaven's sake don't go and destroy everyone's peace of mind.'

'Meaning what?'

Norris looked at him with ill-concealed impatience. 'Meaning, most people have a few skeletons hidden away in cupboards and that's the best place for them to be. The last thing Mother or any of us want is having you digging them up for public exhibition. Surely you must see the danger?'

Richard remained thoughtful while Norris watched him with a small imperious frown.

'What reason have you for suggesting that Dad may have something hidden in his past?'

'You really are very naïve for a police officer. I just hope you'll be circumspect.'

'Certainly I'll try to be. Moreover, I'll be happy to keep you in touch with the course of my investigations. That is, if you want to be kept in touch.'

'I can see that nothing's going to deter you,' Norris observed with a sniff. 'And now I really must dash or Joanna'll wonder what on earth's happened to me.'

'Any message for Mum?'

'I did see her this morning at the funeral,' Norris replied loftily. 'And I've told her to let me know when she hears from the solicitors about probate of Father's will. She'll need some advice at that stage.'

'Isn't that what the solicitors are for?' Richard enquired, though it was obvious that the irony was lost on his brother.

'A second opinion won't come amiss. Of course you know he's left her everything.'

'I know. It's what I'd have expected anyway.'

'It means she ought to make a fresh will as soon as possible.'

Richard nodded vaguely. He wasn't interested in his father's estate, still less in his mother's testamentary intentions, though they obviously occupied Norris' thoughts.

He decided he would discuss Norris' views with Sophie on the way to his mother's flat, in particular his reservations about Richard's proposed investigation.

'I think you should go ahead,' Sophie said when he told her, as they edged their way along in the rush hour traffic.

'I'm glad.'

'You're certainly not going to be happy if you don't.'

'Is that the only reason you agree?'

'No. I think you owe it to the memory you hold of your father. It may be that the mystery will remain unsolved at the end, but at least you'll have the satisfaction of having tried.'

'But I shall solve it. I'm determined to.'

'I hope so, but be prepared for a not necessarily happy ending.'

He brought the car to a halt outside the block of flats where his mother lived. Letting his hands rest on the steering wheel, he said, 'Why do you say that?'

'If your father had wanted anyone to know why he was taking his life, don't you think he'd have left a note? After all, most suicides do. You've told me that yourself.'

'It's true, but I can't believe that Dad's failure to provide an explanation means he had some reason he didn't ever want revealed.'

'But it is a possibility. Why not ask your mother and be guided by her view?'

He leaned across and kissed her. 'You're a bright girl and the sooner I marry you the better.'

Sophie, whose last name was Piper, was just twenty and lived at home with a widower father and two younger sisters who were still at school. Her mother had died when Sophie was fifteen and for a time she had run the house. But now there was a part-time housekeeper who performed most of the basic household chores. Her father, who was the chief engineer at a large modern brewery, had been determined that his older daughter shouldn't be turned into a domestic drudge before she had even left school. Her sisters aged fifteen and ten both adored her and had been quick to adopt her as a mother substitute.

Fay Deegan kissed them both on their arrival and led the way into the living-room.

'You can do the drinks, Richard. I'm afraid I've already started.' She sat down on the sofa and tucked her legs beneath her. 'I'm glad the funeral's over. I found it a great strain.'

'That's not surprising, Mum. Incidentally, I saw Norris this evening. He sent his love.'

He handed Sophie her usual glass of Cinzano Bianco and sat down at the opposite end of the sofa from his mother with a glass of beer in his hand.

'Do you mind if we talk about Dad for a few minutes?' he asked.

'What about him?' His mother's tone was faintly defensive. 'If it's about his estate . . .'

'It's nothing to do with his estate. That's something between you and the solicitors and I've no intention of sticking my nose in.'

'I'm sorry, Richard, but I thought Norris might have said something to you. I shall certainly let you both know as soon as I hear from the lawyers because there'll be quite a lot to discuss. For instance, whether I should go on living in this flat.'

'Why on earth not?' Richard exclaimed in a startled tone.

'I'm not saying I shan't, but it'll depend on how I'm placed financially when everything's been finally sorted out.'

Richard blinked at her in surprise. He had never been aware of any shortage of money in the family. Admittedly, his father's enormous earnings at the Bar would quickly dry up, but he must surely have saved quite a bit. Moreover, his mother had a private income of her own. Nothing spectacular but, as far as he knew, enough to keep a fairly robust wolf from the door.

'Anyway, I may want to move,' his mother went on, observing his expression.

'That's different. I could understand that. Though it's a jolly nice flat,' he added, gazing fondly about him.

'So what was it you wanted to say about Dad?' she asked as he returned his gaze to her.

'Have you any idea at all, Mum, why he did it?'

'None. You know that.'

'But you must have been thinking about it?'

'I've lain awake every night thinking of nothing else.'

'And still you have no glimmer of an idea?'

'No.'

'Would you like to know why he killed himself?'

'What are you trying to tell me, Richard?'

'But would you . . . would you really like to know, whatever the answer?'

She shifted her gaze and stared in deep thought at the arrangement of coloured grasses in the fireplace.

'I'm not sure,' she said in a distant voice. 'Sometimes it's better not to know everything about somebody one loves. But why are you asking me such questions?'

'Because I want to know what drove Dad to take his life. I shan't be happy until I've found out the reason. And you're the only person who could stop me.'

'Me?'

'If you felt the risks were too great. The risks to your peace of mind.'

'I have no peace of mind. How could I have? When the man you've lived with for twenty-seven years suddenly kills himself without explanation, he destroys your peace of mind as well. Do you think I've not searched every corner of my soul to discover whether I bear any responsibility for what happened! Don't you think that's what fills my thoughts day and night!'

'I'm sorry, Mum,' Richard said in an abject tone as he moved along the sofa and took her hand. 'I didn't mean to distress you. It's just that I know what I want to do, provided it won't upset you.'

'I'm happy that you should. After all, you don't have to tell me anything you think I'd sooner not hear.' She gave his hand a squeeze and jumped up. 'I must go and get the supper out of the oven.'

'I'll come and give you a hand,' Sophie said, following her out of the room.

Going across to the drinks tray, Richard poured himself another beer. It had taken others to foresee possible dangers in his quest. He had always idolised his father and so it hadn't occurred to him that an investigation into his death could turn up anything to his discredit. But Sophie had helped to put the matter in perspective for him. His determination remained, nevertheless, unimpaired.

After the supper dishes had been cleared away, his mother brought in coffee. Conversation during the meal had been kept light and his mother's mood had become more cheerful. She had been entertained by Sophie's description of some of the girls in the typing pool where she worked.

'What about a liqueur, Mum?' Richard said when they had returned to the sitting-room.

'I'll have a brandy. What about you, Sophie?'

'Have you got the one that tastes of orange?'

'Cointreau,' Richard said. 'Sophie only knows them by their flavours, like ice-creams. Peppermint, cherry, cough mixture etcetera.' He poured himself another beer and brought the drinks over. 'Did Dad ever mention the Official Secrets Act case in which he was due to defend?' he asked as he sat down.

'Nothing that I recall. I knew he had the brief because his name had appeared in the newspapers. One of us may have made some comment or other, but it was certainly not anything memorable.'

'He didn't seem troubled by the prospect?'

'No. It was just another case. Your father was a complete professional where his work was concerned. He gave of his best and didn't let his personal views intrude.'

'Were any of his cases preying on his mind at all?' Richard asked.

'He was worried about the one that finished . . .' She bit her lip and went on in a faintly tremulous tone, 'the one that finished his last day. He had been up till nearly three in the morning working on it. He said that unless he could persuade the judge on some technical point, his client faced a long stretch

41

in prison. I know he felt a heavy responsibility on his shoulders, but there was nothing new about that.'

'I always had the impression that he carried his responsibilities fairly lightly.'

'He wasn't given to agonising after a case was over, but that didn't mean he didn't feel the weight of responsibility while it was going on.'

As he listened to his mother, Richard began to wonder if he might not be barking up the wrong tree. Perhaps his father's death was not connected with any of his cases. The fact remained, however, that it followed his inexplicable *volte-face* over the Official Secrets Act case. Why had he suddenly refused to defend Peter Kulka? And announced his decision in such uncompromising fashion?

Richard would dearly have liked to know whether his father had made or received any telephone calls after Stanley had left Chambers. But there was no way of finding out. In any event, one had to remember that he had behaved out of character before Stanley's departure which made it unlikely that a subsequent telephone call had triggered the decision to end his life. It seemed more likely that fateful decision had been reached between leaving the Old Bailey and arriving back in his room at Chambers. According to Stanley, all they had talked about was the case he had just triumphantly finished, the Peter Kulka case and the brief delivered that afternoon to defend Terence Edward-Jones.

'I don't suppose you knew, Mum,' Richard remarked, 'that Dad had been asked to defend the son of Tom Edward-Jones, the property millionaire.'

'That horrible man!' She gave a small shudder.

'I don't suppose he's any worse than others of his ilk.'

'He's the only millionaire I've ever met and that was enough.'

'Do you mean you know him?' Richard asked in surprise.

'I've not seen him for years, but there was a time when one could scarcely open a paper without reading about him.'

'Did Dad know him?'

'I'd never have met him on my own,' she said in an indignant tone. 'He and your father met in the army during their national service in Germany. He tried to keep in touch afterwards, but

Laurence never cared for him and did his best to shake off such ies as had existed. He married a perfectly terrible girl, too. The worst type of brassy barmaid. We simply had nothing in common.'

Richard digested this item of information in silence for a while. Do you know when Dad was last in touch with him?' he asked at length.

Fay frowned. 'He used to phone occasionally. The last time was several weeks ago. Your father was out and he said he'd call again later. He didn't leave his name, but I recognised his voice.'

'Did you tell Dad?'

'No, I didn't. I saw no need to in the circumstances.' She paused. 'If his son's anything like him, I'm not surprised he's in trouble with the police.'

'That's a bit of an understatement. After all murder is murder. But it may explain why his father was so keen to have Dad defend him. He'd obviously followed Dad's career and wanted the best advocate he could get for his son's defence.'

'I don't imagine Laurence would have been very pleased at the prospect.'

It was shortly after this that Fay began to show signs of tiredness and Richard and Sophie took their leave.

'I have a rest day tomorrow,' he said as he drove Sophie home, 'so I can get cracking first thing.'

He stopped the car short of her house and switched off the engine, before pulling her in to his side for what her younger sister referred to with brazen curiosity as a snogging session. It had been the discovery of Kate, the sister in question, secretly watching them through a crack in her bedroom curtains that had obliged them to park away from the house.

'You'd have thought she'd have seen enough of that sort of thing on the box,' Sophie had remarked when they had first made the discovery.

'Real life always provides a more exciting show,' Richard had replied with a grin. 'I bet she's told all her school-friends too.'

'The little peeping tom!'

But if there was one thing Katie knew, it was how to get round her eldest sister.

CHAPTER VI

Richard's first move the next morning was to call Stanley.

'Do you happen to know whether Mr Edward-Jones ever rang my father in Chambers?'

'Mr Tom Edward-Jones, do you mean?'

'Yes.'

'He wouldn't have spoken to him direct, only through his son's solicitor.'

'I understand they knew each other slightly.'

'I wasn't aware of that.'

'Dad never mentioned him?'

'Never.'

'Would it have been possible for him to have spoken to Dad without your knowing?'

'Certainly. Sometimes your father would ask for an outside line and then dial his own call.'

'But could incoming calls be put through to him without your knowing who was at the other end?'

'Very rarely. Occasionally somebody would ask to speak to your father privately and would decline to give a name.'

'And you'd put them through?'

'Only if your father agreed to take the call.'

'Would he usually agree?'

'It happened so very rarely . . . I know that once or twice he insisted on my finding out who it was. Otherwise I was to say he wasn't available. But there was the odd occasion when he agreed to take the call. I always assumed it was because he guessed who the caller was.'

'Can you remember any such calls having an effect on him?'

'No, I can't pretend that I do.'

'And you've no recollection of any calls from Mr Edward-Jones?'

'No. That I'm sure about. I'd have remembered his name. I had no idea they knew each other.'

'I gather it was a long time ago. My mother says they knew one another in the army just after the war, but that they were never close friends.'

'That would have been before your father was called to the Bar.'

'Yes. He went straight into the army from school in 1948. He didn't go to Cambridge until two years later.'

'I'm afraid I'll have to ring off, Richard. Half Chambers seem to be clamouring for my attention.'

Twenty minutes later, Richard found himself outside the offices of Messrs Weinstock & Walper in a side street not far from Olympia. From a quick enquiry, he knew them to be a small, busy and respectable firm, even if they had a tendency to become involved in cases with a political flavour. The Queen against Peter Kulka certainly fell into that category.

Richard had barely stepped over their threshold before deciding that one way they didn't spend their profits was on giving their premises a face-lift. There was well-worn brown linoleum on the floor and a pervading smell of fustiness. It would not have surprised him to find a large sepia photograph of Queen Victoria gazing at him from the wall. He walked across to a hatch which bore the inscription 'Enquiries' in black letters on its frosted glass and jabbed his finger on a bell-push at the side.

The glass panel was slid back and a narrow female face filled the space.

'Can I help you?' she asked in a gushy tone which didn't seem to go with either the surroundings or her austere appearance.

'I'd like to speak to Mr Weinstock.'

'Is he expecting you?'

'No. My name's Richard Deegan. I'm the son of Mr Laurence Deegan, the Q.C.'

'Take a seat and I'll find out if Mr Weinstock can see you.'

There was a wooden bench against the farther wall and Richard went and sat on it. It was as unyielding as it looked.

He didn't have long to wait, however, before a door opened and another middle-aged female appeared. This one wore spectacles which were attached to a chain round her neck so that they rested on her bosom when not in use.

'You wish to see Mr Weinstock?'

'Yes. I promise not to keep him long.'

'I'm sure he'll give you all the time he feels necessary,' she said reprovingly. 'If you'll come this way . . .'

Richard followed her through the door into a short corridor that was so dark he instinctively put out a hand to guide himself.

'I'm afraid the light bulb is broken,' the severe voice said. 'We're waiting for a new one.' She spoke as if it was a major undertaking and might not be accomplished for weeks. It probably wouldn't either, Richard reflected.

She opened a door and stood aside for him to enter. A small rotund man with a bald head and fluffed out hair at the sides stood up.

'Mr Deegan? I'm Leonard Weinstock. Terrible tragedy your father's death. A great loss to the Bar and to the future Bench. Very glad to have this opportunity of expressing my condolences to a member of the family. Do sit down, Mr Deegan and tell me what I can do for you.'

'It's very kind of you to see me without an appointment, sir, and I can tell you quite simply why I've come. My father, as you may be aware, left no note explaining his death, but I've decided to try and discover what caused him to take his life.'

'I see. Or rather I understand, though I don't see that I can help you.'

'You had sent him the defence brief in the case of Peter Kulka.'

'I had, indeed. I couldn't think of a better person to defend that muddled man. I speak in confidence, of course, but that's just what he is, a muddled young man. Though that's very different from saying he's guilty of an offence under the Official Secrets Act.' Mr Weinstock made a gesture resembling an episcopal blessing. 'I've now sent the brief to Mr Colino, another fine advocate, though between ourselves I wouldn't quite put him in your father's class. I know Stanley would have liked me

46

to have left the brief in his Chambers, but I thought it wiser in all the circumstances to take it elsewhere.' He paused and frowned suddenly. 'Forgive my asking, but are you the son who's at the Bar or the other one?'

'I'm the other one. I'm in the Metropolitan Police.'

'A fine body of men, even if so many of my clients do, unfortunately, find themselves ranged on the other side.' He gave Richard a twinkling smile. 'But a splendid career for a young man. Which branch are you in?'

'Special Branch.'

'Well, well! Then I must be careful what I say.'

'I assure you I'm not involved in any way in the Kulka case.'

'No, of course not,' Mr Weinstock said, though it seemed to Richard that some of the bonhomie had gone out of his tone.

'Did you have any contact with my father over the case?'

The solicitor's hair seemed to fluff out even further as he shook his head.

'I'd just fixed up a consultation that very day he died.'

'Could there have been anything connected with the case to upset him?'

'Good gracious, no. It was a perfectly straightforward case of its kind. My firm has been involved in a number of them over the years. Of course none of them are entirely straightforward, chiefly because of the obstacles placed in our path by the prosecution. The element of secrecy becomes obsessive and half the witnesses are faceless anonyms. If the security service had its way, the defence would never be told anything at all.' He gave Richard a sly grin. 'It'd probably be made compulsory to plead guilty.'

Although he realised the solicitor was only teasing him, Richard decided not to be drawn. He wondered, however, how Messrs Weinstock & Walper had come to be involved in so many O.S. cases. There weren't all that many and it would be unusual for a single firm to have more than one over a period of years.

'Was it the first time you had briefed my father in that sort of case?' he asked.

'Yes, it was. He seemed particularly suitable for this case. Not merely on account of his professional skill, but, of course, he had the added interest in Czechoslovakia where the whole story began.'

'I don't follow you,' Richard said with a slight catch in his voice. 'As far as I know, my father had no special interest in Czechoslovakia.'

Mr Weinstock looked suddenly embarrassed.

'Oh dear, I hope I've not said anything out of turn. But it was at a reception at the Czech Embassy I first met your father socially. In fact we met there two years running.'

Richard experienced a sudden constriction of all his muscles. What on earth had his father been doing at a party given by an Eastern bloc embassy? How had he come to be invited? Admittedly, he didn't pretend to know about his father's social engagements, but he would have expected to have heard of that particular invitation in subsequent conversation. He presumed his mother would have been invited as well and he would call her as soon as he left the solicitor's office.

'It's just that I wasn't aware he knew anyone at the Czech Embassy,' he said in a hopefully casual tone. 'But there's no earthly reason why I should have known.'

'There were two or three hundred other people present, so it wasn't exactly a clandestine occasion,' Mr Weinstock said with a disarming smile. 'Once you get on their guest lists, I have the impression that only death removes you.' He beamed. 'I also get invited to functions at the Polish and Hungarian embassies, as I'm sure your S.B. records show.'

'I wouldn't know,' Richard said gruffly.

'No need to feel embarrassed, Mr Deegan. I'm not, so why should you be? Think of all the unemployed there would be if the major power blocs disbanded their various intelligence organisations. Tens of thousands would be thrown out of work on both sides of the iron curtain. You might even be yourself.'

'The Special Branch is not an intelligence organisation.'

'No, of course not, but it works very closely with such bodies, does it not?' Mr Weinstock laughed merrily. 'Oh dear, now I've embarrassed you again. My trouble is that I find it hard to take it all seriously.'

Richard rose. He still felt as if he had received a painful kidney punch in the course of the interview.

'I mustn't take up any more of your time, sir. I'm very grateful to you for answering my questions so patiently.'

'It's been my pleasure, Mr Deegan, though I'm sorry that the occasion of our first meeting should have been in such sad circumstances. I certainly wish you success in your quest. For the moment, however, your father's death does, indeed, sound quite baffling.'

He conducted Richard to the barren outer office and waved him goodbye.

At the end of the street, Richard found a telephone kiosk and called his mother. She answered almost immediately.

'I was just on my way out,' she said.

'I'm glad I caught you. This may sound a funny question, Mum, but have you ever been to a party at the Czech Embassy?'

'Where?'

'The Czechoslovakian Embassy.'

'It's a hideous building. It's bad enough passing it in a bus without going inside.'

'So the answer's no?'

'I've never set foot in the place.'

'Did Dad ever mention going there?'

'To the Czech Embassy?' she asked incredulously.

'Yes.'

'I'm sure he never went there in his life. Why are you asking, Richard?'

'I've obviously got hold of the wrong end of the stick,' he said, with a heavy feeling.

'You certainly must have. The only embassies we were ever invited to were the American and the Greek. And once the Singapore High Commission after he had represented them in some case or other.'

'O.K.; thanks, Mum. I'll try and call you this evening.'

Standing on the pavement outside the telephone kiosk, he felt like someone out for an afternoon run who had gone full tilt into a pane of bullet-proof glass. He was mentally bruised and shaken and unsure what to do next. He had brushed aside the warnings he had received and yet even at this early stage it seemed he might be lifting the lid off a Pandora's box.

As he walked slowly down the road toward the nearest tube

station, he wondered whether he should abandon his quest. But then his sense of resolve reasserted itself. Just because his father had attended a couple of receptions at the Czech Embassy didn't mean he had acted discreditably. There could be a dozen reasons why he hadn't mentioned the occasions to his family, none of them of any significance.

Of course he must continue. What was more, he knew whom he would tackle next.

CHAPTER VII

Although it was his rest day, Richard decided to call in at his office at New Scotland Yard. It was a risky thing to do as there was always the danger of being grabbed for duty.

He found a message on his desk in Pat Tinkler's writing. He and Detective Constable Tinkler were of the same age and seniority, but otherwise as different as Starsky from Hutch.

The message said that a Mr Edward-Jones had been trying to get in touch with him and would be obliged if he would call him back as soon as possible. Pat Tinkler had written down the number and added the comment, 'He said it was a private matter. Probably wants to give you an apartment block in Mayfair.'

Richard stuffed the piece of paper in his pocket and made a quick telephone call before slipping away again. Mr Edward-Jones could wait.

Twenty minutes later he arrived at the Law Courts and asked for directions to Mr Justice Hensley's room. It was half-way along a corridor of solid doors, on the wall beside each of which was painted the name of the room's occupant in bold black letters.

Richard knocked and was immediately bidden to enter. Mr Justice Hensley's ermine-trimmed robe was thrown across a chair and the judge was putting on his jacket as Richard opened the door.

'Hello, Uncle Sam,' he said with a hopeful smile.

The judge had been Uncle Sam to both Norris and himself since they were children, though since his call to the Bar his brother had taken to addressing him with affected formality as 'judge'.

'How are you, Richard? Didn't have a chance to speak to you properly at the funeral. And how's your mother?'

'Pretty well considering what she's been through.'

'I plan to get in touch with her shortly about a memorial service for your father. I've spoken to the Inn about it. Probably in about six weeks' time.'

'Oh, I'm delighted to hear that. Norris had hinted that the Benchers might veto the idea because . . . because of Dad having taken his own life.'

Mr Justice Hensley frowned slightly. 'Your brother can be a trifle priggish at times, I'm afraid. And unfortunately the Bar isn't the best place to exorcise that particular trait. But that's not what you've come to talk about.' He glanced at his watch. 'I have to get across to the Inn for lunch in a few minutes. Contrary to popular belief judges don't have three-hour lunch breaks. But I'll be free after Court this afternoon if you like to come back.'

'Thanks, Uncle Sam. All I wanted to tell you was that I'm determined to find out why Dad killed himself. There must have been a reason and my belief is that it's something connected with one of his cases.'

Mr Justice Hensley paused in the act of lighting a cigarette. 'That sounds a bit far-fetched. In my time at the Bar, I've known difficult cases, worrying cases and badly-prepared cases, but never one that made me contemplate suicide. Do you have a particular case in mind?'

'Yes, the Official Secrets Act case in which Dad had been instructed to defend Peter Kulka.'

'I read a bit about it in the newspaper but that's all I know.'

'Dad had had the brief for about a couple of weeks without looking at it and then on the day he committed suicide, he suddenly told Stanley to return it. It came right out of the blue and he wouldn't give Stanley any explanation. Stanley tried to talk him round, but he appeared adamant and a few hours later we all know what he did.'

Mr Justice Hensley was thoughtful for a few seconds. 'I had, of course, heard about him wanting to return that brief. The

52

whole Temple was awash with rumours for a few days after his death and I went along to see Stanley myself and he told me. I'm bound to say, Richard, that he didn't associate the brief with your father's death and I would agree with him.'

'Stanley isn't aware of what I've now found out.'

'And that is?'

'That Dad had ties of some sort with the Czechoslovak Embassy.'

'I think you ought to explain that remark,' the judge said with a certain judicial severity.

Richard related the details of his visit that morning to the offices of Messrs Weinstock & Walper.

'Attending a couple of receptions isn't exactly having ties,' the judge remarked in a neutral tone. 'You made it sound somewhat tendentious.'

'I'm sorry, I didn't mean to. But you have to admit, Uncle Sam, that it's very odd that Mum knew nothing of his visits.'

'Hmm.' For what seemed an age to Richard, Mr Justice Hensley stared at him with a thoughtful expression. 'Your father used to have left-wing leanings as a young man, but I thought he'd grown out of them,' he said at last.

'I'd always regarded him as being fairly non-political,' Richard remarked. 'When he did comment on a current issue, he sounded pretty middle of the road. Though I do remember once when Mum was going to put a Conservative poster in the window at one election, he asked her not to, as he didn't wish to wear a public label of any sort.'

'I certainly never heard him express any strong political views in recent years,' Mr Justice Hensley agreed. 'I was thinking back to the time when he joined Chambers as a pupil in the early 'fifties. He was just down from Cambridge and was said to have dabbled in left-wing politics there. Except that dabbled is a bit of a euphemism. Of course, those were still unsettled years after the war. Moreover, that's what a university is for, to indulge one's excesses and eccentricities and get them out of one's system.'

'Are you saying, Uncle Sam, that he brought politics into Chambers with him.'

'No, I'm not, Richard, because he never did anything of the sort.' He paused. 'I'd never have known anything had it not been for the fact that Professor Owen North, who was your father's law tutor at Cambridge, was an old friend of mine. We'd been contemporaries at university and have been life-long friends since. Indeed, it was he who directed your father's footsteps to Mulberry Court. He thought extremely highly of him and believed he was destined to have an outstanding career.'

'Is Professor North still alive, Uncle Sam?'

'Alas, he died last year. But I don't think he and your father ever kept in close touch.'

A silence fell, broken by Richard who said in a suddenly bleak tone, 'Do you think I'm going to regret embarking on this quest, Uncle Sam?' When the judge didn't immediately answer, he went on, 'I've barely begun, but already I've been given cause to wonder. After all, if my curiosity leads me to turn up things better left hidden, nobody's going to thank me and I'm not going to like myself very much.'

'You're not obliged to reveal anything you find out.'

'That, in effect, is what Mum said.'

The judge nodded. 'You, presumably, wouldn't tell her anything you felt would distress her?'

'No, I wouldn't.'

'I'm glad to hear that. I'm a great believer in not telling people things that would upset them if they don't need to know.'

'I agree, Uncle Sam.'

'In that event, provided you yourself are prepared to face something disagreeable and will keep it under your hat, there's no reason why you shouldn't pursue your private enquiries. How far you get is another matter.'

'Do you think I *shall* be faced with something disagreeable as you put it?'

Mr Justice Hensley let out a sigh. 'I knew your father for over twenty-five years. I held him in high esteem and enjoyed his company on all occasions. Obviously I'd like to believe that he has nothing discreditable in his background, but there aren't many men who've led utterly unblemished lives. It all depends on the nature of the blemish. Most of us have things in our past, maybe nothing more than a peccadillo or two, which we would sooner people didn't know about.' He fixed Richard with a steady look. 'As you yourself have said, there has to be some

54

explanation of your father's action, but the fact that he didn't leave a note of any kind does suggest he doesn't want the world to know it.'

'In that case, have I the right to go burrowing into his life? May I not end up destroying my memory of him?'

'You were very fond of him, weren't you?'

'I adored him.'

'Could what made him so wonderful to you be expunged by discovery of something terrible about him?'

Richard furrowed his brow. 'I can't think of anything terrible.'

'Supposing you found out that he had been a Russian agent all these years or supposing you discovered he had committed some beastly crime as a young man and had lived with the knowledge ever since, would you feel betrayed? Would you feel that what you'd found out negated everything that made him such a wonderful father to you?'

Richard shook his head in a bewildered manner. 'Surely my answer must be no. I might feel shaken and upset, but it couldn't alter all he did for me as a father. That's indelibly recorded on the credit side. Nothing can erase it. I suppose I might feel differently if he'd lavished expensive presents on me and I later found out he had stolen the money to buy them, but it wasn't that sort of relationship. He was a wonderful father in what he gave me in the way of love and help and understanding. Whether he was a Russian agent or a rapist, or something worse than either, can't affect that.' In a decisive tone, he added, 'Nothing can diminish my memory of him.'

'Then you've answered your own question,' Mr Justice Hensley remarked in an impartial tone. 'Hope for the best, but be prepared for something less. And good luck.'

'I'm afraid I've made you terribly late for your lunch, Uncle Sam,' Richard said, glancing at his watch and jumping up.

'I rather think you've caused me to forfeit it altogether. But it'll do me no harm to go without a meal. My tummy may rumble a bit in court this afternoon, but it'll probably be mistaken for one of the antiquated radiators which can make very human noises at times.'

'I'm terribly grateful to you for listening to me.'

'If talking has helped you to see things in clearer perspective,

I'm delighted to have been of service. And remember, I'm always
here, Richard. I'm not asking you to commit yourself, but if
you do discover anything that disturbs you, don't hesitate to
come along and have a talk.'

'Thanks, Uncle Sam. I'm sure I shall want to do that.'

'Incidentally, does Norris know what you're up to?'

'Yes, and he's faintly disapproving.'

'I can well believe that,' Mr Justice Hensley remarked drily

'Has he appeared in front of you yet?' Richard asked with a
grin.

'No. And it's not a day to which I particularly look forward.
Where does he get that expression of frowning disapproval with
which he's apt to greet everything? Certainly not from your
father or mother.'

'He's supposed to be like Mum's father.'

'Of course! He was a Presbyterian minister, wasn't he?'

Richard nodded. 'Poor Mum had a very strict upbringing.
The only book she was allowed to read on Sundays was her
Bible and all her dolls were locked away in a cupboard. It's not
surprising she left home as soon as she could, though she didn't
get married until after her father's death. She's four years older
than Dad was.'

After his visitor had gone, Mr Justice Hensley tried to remember what he knew of Richard's own origins. He recalled that he
had been adopted when only a few weeks old and when Norris
was two. He didn't believe he had ever heard who Richard's
parents had been, though presumably Laurence and Fay had
known.

In any event, it was inconceivable that the explanation of
Laurence Deegan's suicide lay in that direction.

CHAPTER VIII

Richard crossed the road and entered one of the public houses frequented by the Temple's denizens. It was a quarter to two and the worst of the midday rush was over, though the place was still fairly full. He reached the counter by squeezing between the backs of two well-padded barristers who were the centre of respective groups. He regarded it as anti-social to occupy counter space once one's order had been filled and had no compunction about elbowing his way between them.

As soon as he had been served, he withdrew to a far corner to drink his pint of beer and eat a roast beef sandwich. He glanced around, but didn't see anyone he knew, which was hardly surprising seeing that it was away from his normal scene. He wondered whether Norris ever used this particular pub.

He was about to depart when the door opened and a couple of young men came in, one of whom he immediately recognised as Mark, Stanley's junior assistant. His companion thrust his way to the bar counter, leaving Mark just inside the door. Mark's face broke into a friendly smile as he spotted Richard and he came over.

'Hi Not seen you in here before.'

'It's not my usual beat I just happened to be in the area and dropped in for a quick snack That's not John with you, is it?'

'No, he's holding the fort back in Chambers.'

'I didn't think it was, but I haven't seen him for some time and only caught a fleeting glimpse of the chap with you.'

'He's Tony from the Chambers on the ground floor. We

57

usually have to wait until everyone else has had lunch and returned. That's why we're always late.'

'How's Stanley?' Richard enquired, for want of anything else to say.

'He looks after himself at lunchtime all right,' Mark observed in a knowing tone. 'He and one or two other senior clerks get together. A bit like a meeting of the Mafia.'

At this point, Mark's companion arrived back precariously balancing two plates of food on top of the mugs of beer he was carrying. Richard decided to make his departure before he could be drawn into further conversation.

He re-crossed the road and entered one of the telephone kiosks outside the Law Courts. Glancing at the piece of paper he took from his pocket, he dialled the number Tom Edward-Jones had left.

'E. J. Properties Limited,' a voice announced after a minimum of ringing.

'I'd like to speak to Mr Edward-Jones.'

'I'll put you through to his secretary,' the voice replied crisply.

A second later, an equally crisp voice said, 'Mr Edward-Jones' office.'

'My name's Richard Deegan. I believe Mr Edward-Jones was trying to call me this morning.'

'Detective Constable Deegan of the Special Branch, would that be?'

'Yes.'

'Hold the line a moment, Mr Deegan, and I'll find out if Mr Edward-Jones is in his room.'

You know bloody well he is, Richard had a strong urge to tell her. Instead in a tone to match her own, he said, 'I'm in a public call box and I don't have any more coins.' It wasn't true, but let that be her worry.

'You had better give me your number, Mr Deegan, and remain in the box if we get cut off,' she replied without hesitation.

One had to hand it to her, he reflected. Presumably one didn't get to be a millionaire's secretary unless one was beyond being disconcerted by life's minor rubs. With a resigned sigh he fished two more coins from his pocket.

It was not many seconds, however, before another voice came on the line. Male, warm and friendly.

'Mr Deegan? This is Tom Edward-Jones. We've never met, but I'd very much like to rectify that. Would you be free to meet me for a drink this evening?'

'What time?'

'Six o'clock suit you?'

'Yes, I can manage that.'

'Great! Do you know the Croesus Club in Curzon Street?'

'I'm afraid not.'

'I thought the police knew everywhere,' he said with a laugh. 'But perhaps it reflects well on my club that you don't know it.' From his tone Richard was uncertain whether he meant the club of which he was a mere member or the club which he owned. Edward-Jones now went on, 'It's the Park Lane end of the street. It'll be a good place for a quiet drink. I'll see you there at six o'clock. Incidentally, I'll leave word at the door so they'll be expecting you.'

As he stepped out of the kiosk into the fresh air, two things passed through Richard's mind. First that Tom Edward-Jones obviously knew quite a lot about him and had felt no need to hide the fact. Secondly, and equally obviously, he accepted that Richard must be aware of what he wished to see him about. Though his father's name had not once been mentioned, he must have been uppermost in both their minds.

By the time he arrived outside the Croesus Club about three hours later, he had had a haircut and had given his shoes a polish. The haircut had been part of his plan for the afternoon anyway, but the shoeshine was strictly for the benefit of his host.

The entrance to the club was so discreet that he realised he had passed by it on numerous occasions without observing it. It was sandwiched between two larger buildings whose ostentatious exteriors claimed the eye. The words 'Croesus Club' were printed in small letters on a muted black plate beside the door which was closed. As he approached, it was opened by a young man in bottle-green livery.

'Good evening, sir.'

'Mr Edward-Jones is expecting me.'

'Would you be Mr Deegan?'

'I would.'

The young man stepped aside. 'If you care to leave your coat with me, sir, Linda will take you to Mr Edward-Jones.'

Richard became aware of an attractive girl who had suddenly materialised at his side. She was dressed in a well-cut trouser suit the same colour as the young man's livery.

She led the way along a short, thickly carpeted corridor, turning through a narrow archway at the end. Richard paused on the threshold to adjust his vision, for the room ahead was so discreetly lit as to resemble a cinema after the lights have been extinguished. Against a delicate glow on the far side, he could discern a bar There were one or two pools of subdued light elsewhere in the room, but they were being avoided as if they were radioactive.

A figure loomed up in front of him.

'Mr Deegan? How nice to meet you! I'm Tom Edward-Jones. Let me get you a drink. What would you like?'

'A vodka and tonic, please.'

His host led the way to a banquette seat in a corner of the room As they sat down, a barman came over.

'A large vodka and tonic for my guest, Len, and I'll have my usual.'

'Lime or lemon with your vodka, sir?' Len enquired.

'Oh . . . er .   lime, I think,' Richard said, recovering from surprise.

'I much prefer lime, too,' Edward-Jones remarked. 'Trouble is that one is rarely given the choice in this country It is another thing in the Croesus Club's favour.'

'I'm sure there are others,' Richard observed, peering slowly about him until his gaze came finally to rest on his host's face. It was a handsome face with a firm mouth and eyes which never seemed to flicker. He had thick, dark, curly hair with a few touches of grey which might almost have been added by a make-up artist.

Len, the barman, returned with their drinks and placed dishes of fat black olives and roasted almonds on the table before melting away again.

'Cheers,' Tom Edward-Jones said, raising a glass which looked as if it contained cough mixture. 'By the way, may I call you Richard?'

'Please do.'

Edward-Jones put down his glass and reached for an olive with a well-manicured hand on one finger of which was a heavy gold signet ring.

'I'm not someone normally at a loss for words, but I find it a bit hard to explain exactly why I wanted to meet you, Richard. Partly because I was very shocked to read about your father's death and wanted to express my personal condolences to one of the family' He paused and scanned Richard's face as if to assess the effect of his words.

'It came as a terrible shock to all of us.'

'I'm sure it must have done. And do you still have no idea why he did it?'

'None. But I intend to find out.'

'Am I right in assuming you're aware that I knew your father?'

'You were in the army together, weren't you?'

'Yes. We were second lieutenants in the same unit in Germany. It seems like a long time ago. It *was* a long time ago. It was when conditions were still pretty chaotic in that country. Before it achieved its economic miracle.'

Richard nodded slowly. He was still wondering why he had been bidden so urgently to the plush ambience of the Croesus Club.

'Used your father to talk much about those times?' Edward-Jones went on.

'Not really,' Richard said cautiously. 'After all it was only a brief interlude in his life.'

'True,' he remarked and fell silent for several further seconds. 'Look, Richard, I don't wish to embarrass you by my questions, but you've said you were aware we knew each other, was that as a result of his talking about me?'

Richard reached for his glass and took a long swig. The fact was that the question did embarrass him and he wasn't sure how to answer it. He was even beginning to wish he hadn't come.

'No, my mother told me,' he said uncomfortably.

'Your mother?' Tom Edward-Jones sounded surprised. 'I didn't think she allowed my name to pass her lips. I'm sorry, I

61

shouldn't have said that. But it was because of your mother that your father and I ceased to keep in touch. This is going back a good many years, but she and my then-wife didn't get on and she also made it clear that she didn't really approve of me.' He let out a small, false laugh. 'She was probably right. I've always been a bit of a vulgarian.' He shot Richard a quizzical look. 'Does that tally with what she's told you about me?'

Richard took further refuge in his drink before replying. 'Actually, it was only the other day, since my father's death, that she mentioned you'd known each other.'

'Ah! Until then you'd been unaware of my existence?'

'I wouldn't exactly say that,' Richard replied with a faint smile. 'One can't read newspapers and remain unaware of your existence.'

'May I ask how my name cropped up?'

'I happened to say something to my mother about a brief that had been sent to my father to defend someone called Edward-Jones.'

'I follow,' he said in a heavily pensive tone. His eyes, which had hitherto danced with life, suddenly gave him a sad and defeated air. But the look was transitory.

'Your father was going to defend my son.'

'I know.'

'He's been charged with murder. He was out with some girl and she died on him. Dropped dead in the middle of a youthful sexual frolic. He's only twenty and the last thing he intended was to hurt her. He wouldn't hurt anyone. I know your father could have got him off. I was looking forward to working with him on the case. You know what I mean, supplying him with any ammunition he wanted. I've already lined up a couple of doctors who'll say the girl died of vagal inhibition. You'll know more about that than I do, but I gather it means she could have collapsed and died if a feather had brushed against her neck. Well, not literally a feather, but with only a minimum of pressure on her neck.'

'Is she supposed to have been strangled?'

'Yes, which is bloody ridiculous. Why should he have strangled her when all he was wanting was a roll in the hay?'

Richard refrained from pointing out that a good many girls

lost their lives in those precise circumstances. If young Edward-Jones was anything like his father, he could imagine a strong streak of latent violence in his make-up.

'I gather the brief only arrived in Chambers on the very afternoon of my father's death,' Richard remarked.

'You're not suggesting the two events are connected, I hope.' The tone was challenging.

'Lord, no! How could they have been?'

'Exactly.' He half-raised a hand and the barman appeared suddenly at their table. 'Same again please, Len.'

The barman gathered up their glasses, moved silently away and returned in no time with fresh drinks. Edward-Jones appeared preoccupied and Richard once more fell to contemplating the strange nature of their meeting. Whatever had been its real purpose, it had the stamp of a non-event.

As if reading his thoughts, Edward-Jones said abruptly, 'You may still be wondering why I wanted to meet you. It's true that I wanted to tell you how sorry I am about your father's death, but I confess that I was also curious to find out whether he had talked about our days together in the army. In short, I wondered how well you might feel you knew me.' He smiled ruefully. 'Now I have the answer. Not at all. You see, if your father had talked about me, you'd have wondered why I never got in touch after his death, particularly when you knew he was going to defend my Terry. But now I know I was a non-person in your household. A never-mentioned name. Mind you, I'm still delighted to have met you, but I owed you, at least, that word of explanation. Otherwise you'd have gone away wondering why on earth I'd called you and invited you here this evening.'

'When did you last see my father?' Richard asked.

'It must have been ten years ago. We happened to meet at a dinner.'

'But you've been in touch with him since then?'

'You sounded just like a police officer when you said that.' Richard shrugged and Edward-Jones went on, 'Anyway, the answer is, yes I have. From time to time I've spoken to him on the phone. I've always hoped we might get together again, but I'm afraid he wasn't interested in resuming our early friendship.

He never said so as bluntly as that, but the message was there all the same.'

'Forgive my asking, but why were you so keen to see him again? After all, you had gone your separate ways and you no longer moved in the same circles.'

From the sudden hardening of his host's expression, Richard thought he was going to be slapped down for his impertinence. Indeed, Tom Edward-Jones gave the impression of wrestling with his thoughts before replying. Eventually, however, he sighed and said, 'I don't know about you, but I'm a gregarious sort of bloke. I like people. I like having them around me. I don't like losing friends. I'd always admired your father and wasn't a bit surprised when he reached the top of his particular tree. I used to follow his cases in the papers, so it was quite natural to try and resume our friendship. And when my son found himself in trouble, your father was the first person I thought of. I was determined that Terry should have the best barrister that money could buy. You understand that, don't you?'

'Did it ever occur to you that Dad might feel embarrassed defending your son in view of all the circumstances?'

'My son needed the best defence and your father was the person to provide it. It was as simple as that.' His tone was tough and uncompromising. How did one reconcile someone who had become a millionaire and who, from all accounts, was quite ruthless with the person who spoke sentimentally about losing friends? Richard gathered that Tom Edward-Jones' progress to the top had not exactly been marked by happy people strewing flowers in his path. Those who had found themselves in his way were more likely to have been trampled underfoot.

In an ostentatious gesture, Edward-Jones now looked at his watch and then drained his glass. Richard, who had no desire to prolong their meeting, stood up.

'Thanks for the drinks,' he said. 'I've enjoyed meeting you.'

'And I've enjoyed meeting you, too, Richard,' his host said, once more benign. 'Can I offer you a lift? My chauffeur's outside with the car.'

'No, thanks. I've got mine parked not far away.'

As they walked toward the archway which led into the passage, Richard felt an arm go round his shoulders.

'It's probably presumptuous of me, Richard, but I'm going to offer you a word of advice. Advice which I'm sure your Dad would have given you Forget the past. There's never anything to be achieved by raking it over. If he'd wanted you to know why he took his life, he could easily have left a note. But he didn't and my advice would be to accept the situation.'

Richard shook off, as tactfully as he could, the arm which encircled his shoulders. 'I've already received much the same advice,' he said. 'I've thought about it, but I'm still going ahead.'

Tom Edward-Jones allowed his arm to fall to his side like a broken wing.

'Then all I can do is wish you luck. You'll probably need it.'

As they arrived at the entrance, the young man in green livery came forward with Richard's coat and helped him on with it. Richard was fumbling in his pocket for a coin when he observed his host slip the young man a £1 note. As they stepped out on to the pavement, a Mercedes glided up and a chauffeur jumped out.

'Sure I can't give you a lift?'

'No, thanks.'

Tom Edward-Jones held out his hand. 'I hope we'll meet again, Richard.'

With a nod of farewell, Richard turned and walked off along the pavement. He couldn't help wondering who had been fooling whom. Was he really expected to believe that Tom Edward-Jones' prime consideration had been in offering his condolences? No, the really interesting thing was that he had taken the trouble to seek out Richard at all. He must have had a good reason for doing so and to have given up an hour of his expensive time entertaining him.

And with what result? For Richard, it had merely served to arouse his suspicions and reinforce his determination to pursue his enquiries. And for Tom Edward-Jones? That was something Richard would dearly have liked to know.

CHAPTER IX

The effect of Richard kissing her was always to make Sophie feel light-headed. She surrendered herself totally to his embraces and it took her time afterwards to retrieve her thinking processes.

'You're not listening, my love,' he said.

'Yes, I am.'

'You've got your faraway, dreamy look.'

'No, I am listening.'

'Well, what do you think then?'

'I think you have the nicest shaped mouth I've ever seen. And I adore your dimple.'

'Forget my dimple or I'll only ever show you the non-dimple side of my face. Anyway, men shouldn't have dimples. They should vanish with one's milk teeth. If you go on about it, I'll have it surgically removed.'

Sophie sighed. 'I expect I'd still love you. Now you've made me forget what you were asking.'

He gave her another quick kiss. 'Which line of enquiry do you think I should concentrate on?'

'Can't you pursue both at the same time until one elbows the other aside? That's bound to happen sooner or later.'

'You mean, not place a bet until the race is almost over. However, more likely than not, both lines will peter out.'

'You don't really believe that, do you?'

'It could be the case. I may be barking up two completely wrong trees.'

'But you had to start somewhere and you've already uncovered two trails worth following. And it isn't as if you picked them at random. You yourself deduced that your father's death was somehow linked to one of those two cases.'

'But was it a sound deduction?'

'Yes, as has been proved by events. Look what you've already found out!'

'That my father may have been a communist spy or, if not that, caught up with a dubious millionaire.'

'I don't like the sound of Mr Edward-Jones,' Sophie said thoughtfully. 'I think it's very significant that he went to so much trouble to contact you and I don't like it that he seemed to know all about you. How did he find out you were in the police, for example?'

'Dad could have told him, I suppose.' Richard gazed out of the car window. Abruptly he asked, 'Who lives at number forty-nine?'

'I've no idea. Why?'

'I thought I saw somebody peeping at us just now. Perhaps we'd better vary our parking place or the occupants will begin to think they're under surveillance. They'll only have to find out I'm in Special Branch for a real brouhaha to erupt.'

'You can stop outside sixty-three if you're worried. It's empty and up for sale.'

'Katie could see us from there. It's only two away from your house.'

'Even Katie can't see that far in the dark.'

'Your sister is a human radar system.'

'Can't you find out who else served in the same regiment with your father and Mr Edward-Jones?' Sophie asked after a pause. 'If you could trace someone who knew them both in the army, it might help. Isn't there an old photograph lying around at home? Your mother would know, Richard.'

'That's a good idea,' he said, nodding his head in approval. 'I'll call her in the morning.'

But when he did speak to her the next day, he was to draw a blank.

'I'm sure there's nothing of that sort in any of his drawers,' she said. 'Of course, I didn't meet him until he was up at Cambridge, but he never used to talk about his time in Germany. I don't think he enjoyed the army, and once he'd done his service he wanted to forget it. He never kept in touch with any of his army companions, except for that man Edward-Jones, and there it was a question of his thrusting himself at your father.'

'I wonder why he never talked about his time in Germany.'

'I don't think it's all that surprising. Immediately after his military service came Cambridge and the law and he became wholly occupied in carving his career at the Bar. Not to mention acquiring a wife and family. After all, it's not uncommon to meet people who never talk about their schooldays, simply because they didn't enjoy them and put them out of their minds as soon as they could.'

'Have you already sorted out Dad's things in the flat?'

'Yes, and I didn't come across any old army photographs. Anyway, Richard, why are you so interested?'

'Only because it's a bit of a blank in his life and this man, Edward-Jones, has suddenly popped up.'

'What do you mean popped up?'

'He was very keen for Dad to defend his son.'

'So you told me. I'm sure your father would have been rather less keen to take the brief.'

He decided it would be better not to tell his mother how he had come to meet Tom Edward-Jones the previous evening.

Later in the morning, he phoned Norris' Chambers.

'Hello, Norris, I didn't really expect to find you in. I thought you'd probably be in court,' he said in a faintly mischievous tone.

'I had a fixture, but it fell through,' Norris replied, then added self-importantly, 'But it enables me to get on with some paperwork.'

Sorry if I've disturbed your doodling, Richard felt tempted to say, but didn't. Instead he asked, 'Did Dad ever talk to you about his army service?'

'He'd have been more likely to talk to you than to me. All I know is that he was a second lieutenant with an artillery unit in the British Army of Occupation.'

'You never heard him mention the name of any brother officers?'

68

'No. I don't even know the name or number of his unit. I believe he was stationed not far from Hanover, but that's all I can tell you. He was always rather reticent on the subject.'

'That's exactly what I've been thinking. I wonder why.'

'Probably hated every moment of it. Can't really see him as a soldier. Except perhaps as a senior staff officer at some G.H.Q. Now I come to think of it, I do remember when I was about six or seven and going through the toy soldier phase, I once tried to get him to relate his experiences to me, but I got very short shrift. He just said there was nothing to tell and I could spend my time more profitably reading than playing with plastic soldiers.'

'Interesting.'

'What are you up to, Richard?' Norris' tone was suddenly sharp.

'Just nosing around a bit.'

'Well, for God's sake don't go and stir anything up.'

'Don't worry, I won't.'

'I wish I could believe that. The trouble with you policemen is you can't stop poking and prodding.'

'I thought lawyers were also meant to have enquiring minds.'

'Only when we're paid to,' Norris said severely.

'Well, I mustn't keep you from your paperwork.'

'Joanna would like you to come to supper one evening, Richard We must try and fix something up.'

Richard felt reasonably certain that the supper invitation, when it came, would not include Sophie. Some excuse would be found not to ask her. Probably that Joanna needed just the odd man to make up her numbers.

But his mind became occupied with more pressing matters when he rang off. Why had his father been so secretive about his national service? Was it merely in an effort to forget an unenjoyable period of his life or was there some hidden motive? His outburst at Norris for playing with his soldiers was not only curious but out of character. It was as if he didn't want the smallest reminder of his own time in uniform.

On the other hand, was it not also consistent with a strongly held communist-cum-pacifist view? Of one thing Richard was sure, if his father *had* been a secret agent, it would have been for ideological reasons and not for money.

That was a shocking enough thought, but he had already stepped over the threshold of believing his father to have been an innocent victim of someone else's wicked machinations. The past twenty-four hours had seen to that.

CHAPTER X

Richard spent most of the next day writing a report on a Cypriot immigrant who was suspected of being a member of a terrorist cell and not just the harmless *pâtisserie* cook he affected to be. He was nearing the end of his report when Detective Superintendent Alcester, the officer in charge of the Kulka case, put his head round the door.

'Oh, hello Deegan; I'm looking for Sergeant Wiles. Not seen him, have you?'

'Afraid not, sir.'

Superintendent Alcester made to go again, then paused. Turning back, he said, 'Sorry about your father's death. I know how you must feel. My own father committed suicide. Though in his case, there was a reason. He had an incurable cancer – incurable in those days, that is – and decided to end it all quickly before he became a burden to my mother and everyone around him.' He hesitated a moment. 'I gather your father didn't leave any indication as to why he was doing it?'

'None. It's a complete mystery.'

Superintendent Alcester shook his head sympathetically. 'Must make it that much worse for your mother and you.'

'Yes, it does. I expect you knew, sir, that he was due to defend Kulka.'

'I'd heard.'

'It seems possible that his death was in some way connected with the case.'

Alcester gave him a sharp look. 'In what way?'

'I've no idea, sir, but only a few hours before his death, he

71

told his clerk to return the brief as he didn't wish to defend.'

'Oh, that!' Superintendent Alcester sounded relieved. 'Yes, I heard that from the City of London inspector who dealt with his death. Your father's clerk had mentioned it in his statement and the inspector thought I should know.'

'But you clearly don't regard it as significant?'

'As far as I'm concerned, there's nothing in the case which touched upon your father in a personal way.'

'I know I shouldn't ask this, sir, but do you have anything on my father?'

'Do you mean, was he ever of Special Branch interest?' Richard nodded. 'You'd hardly be working here if he had been.'

'I suppose not.'

'No suppose about it. For obvious reasons our entrants are more carefully vetted than most.' He gave Richard a long, shrewd look. 'On the face of it, Deegan, that was an extraordinary question. Why should your father have been in S.B. records?'

Richard felt covered in confusion under the watchful stare of his superior officer. 'I only asked, sir, because of the strange coincidence of his suddenly wanting to return the brief and then killing himself almost immediately afterwards.'

'You think there is what the law calls a *nexus* between the two events?' Alcester said thoughtfully.

'It seems a possibility, sir. That's all I had in mind.'

'You're sure it's only the proximity of the two events that made you ask your question? No other factor comes into it?'

Richard shook his head. He certainly didn't propose to tell Superintendent Alcester of his father's visits to the Czech Embassy. He did wonder, however, whether the security service was aware of them. It wasn't a wholly omniscient organisation, though it liked to foster that belief at times. If it did know, he would expect Special Branch to have been informed, seeing how deeply the security service had been involved in investigating Peter Kulka's betrayal of secrets and how generally sensitive it was about outsiders who were sucked in when cases eventually came to court.

'Do you know anything about Kulka's solicitors, sir?'

'I know about them all right, they're constantly popping up in cases with a Special Branch interest. They represent every left-wing cause that's ever been invented. Leonard Weinstock's as slippery as they come, though he's quite an agreeable old bird in his way.'

'You mean, he doesn't pretend to be what he isn't?'

'I'm certainly not saying that; I wouldn't trust him an inch, but he's pleasant enough to deal with on a personal level. At least he's not one of those humourless fanatics we so often cross swords with in our job. Was it the first time his firm had briefed your father?'

'I gather so from my father's clerk, though they've briefed other members of Chambers before.'

'A year or so ago, they must have kept half the Bar in work when there were all those cases arising out of demonstrations and protest marches. All political, all stirred up by left-wing agitators and all providing rich fodder for Messrs Weinstock and Walper.' He peered quickly round the room again as if to satisfy himself that his quarry had not crawled out from beneath a desk. 'Tell Sergeant Wiles, if you see him, that I want to speak to him,' he said and departed, leaving Richard grateful for the opportunity to talk to him which had fortuitously come his way.

If he wanted to talk to an officer connected with the Edward-Jones case, however, he would have to create the opportunity himself. He knew that it was a W Division case, the girl's body having been found on Wimbledon Common, and it didn't take him long to discover that one of the officers who had been involved in the investigation was a Detective Sergeant Angelo whom he had once met in the course of an enquiry. As luck would have it, Sergeant Angelo was not only at his desk, but actually sounded pleased when Richard announced himself.

'I thought it was probably a local shopkeeper who phones me several times a day about a corruption enquiry I have on my plate. He's an absolute pest. One of those people who expects instant results and imagines that his allegation is the only one you're dealing with. I'd invite him along just to take a look at my desk if I thought I'd ever get rid of him again.'

'Try sending him a photograph instead.'

'That's not a bad idea. I could have a number run off and send them out as acknowledgement cards. Anyway, what can I do for you?'

'I believe you were on the Edward-Jones enquiry?'

'Don't tell me that's sprouted a Special Branch interest!'

'No. This is more a personal call. I don't know whether you read about my father's death . . .'

'Oh, God! The Q.C. you mean? I didn't realise he was your father. Stupid of me. There can't be all that number of Deegans around. The penny should have dropped. I'm sorry.'

'No apologies called for. After all, it could have been a distant relative for all you knew. The thing is that my father had been briefed to defend Terence Edward-Jones, but the brief only arrived on the day of his death. I wondered if you could tell me something about the case.'

'What do you want to know?'

'I think I ought to tell you why I'm interested. My father left no clue as to why he suddenly took his life, but I believe it had to do with one of his cases – possibly that one.'

'But from what you say, he didn't have time to open the brief.'

'True, but there was something funny about the way the case came to him and I've since discovered that he and Edward-Jones senior once vaguely knew each other.'

'He's a tough nut all right. The father, I mean. He created hell when his son was charged and since made it clear to all of us that once Terry's acquitted, he's going to have the Detective Chief Superintendent's guts for golf-ball fillings. That is, if the fraud squad don't catch up with him first. I gather they're investigating some of his deals.'

'Is he so confident that his son will get off?'

'He's more than confident, he's determined. Ruthlessly determined, you might say.'

'And what's your personal view of the case?'

'I doubt whether we shall prove murder, but it's certainly manslaughter. He gave her neck more than a fond squeeze. Fractured her hyoid bone. He's either a young sadist or one of those sexually aggressive youths who get over-excited and become violent in the heat of the moment. Either way, he's a menace.'

'What sort of person is he?'

'I'm probably the wrong person to ask, but in my judgement he's a spoilt brat. Not spoilt in the sense he's been pampered and always given everything he asks for, because I gather he had quite a tough upbringing. But his father obviously idolised him – he's the only child of three marriages – and brought him up to be as selfish and ruthless as himself.'

'Does he resemble his father physically?'

'Same cold eyes, but quite good-looking apart from a silly rosebud mouth. From the fuss his father kicked up when we brought his son in for questioning, you'd think we'd arrested the heir to the throne.'

'I suppose you had. To the Edward-Jones throne, that is. Who was the girl he killed?'

'Lesley Ulbourne. Seventeen years old. Daughter of a school caretaker. He'd met her at a local disco a couple of weeks previously and this was only their second time out together. I suspect she was more attracted by his car and the money he threw around than by him. Poor kid! She mayn't have had much going for her, but she didn't deserve to end up strangled on the edge of a golf course a week after her seventeenth birthday.'

'Did Edward-Jones senior ever mention my father's name in connection with his son's defence?'

'Not in my hearing. He came storming along to the station to try and get his son released – that was shortly before we charged him – and he issued all sorts of threats and said he'd get the finest lawyers in the country to represent him, but he never mentioned any names.'

'Who defended at the magistrates' court?'

'Mr Chalmers, his solicitor. It was a section one committal, so he didn't have anything to do.'

'I'd have expected him to put up a fight at the lower court.'

'Presumably Mr Chalmers advised against and, for once, Tom E-J listened to someone's advice. In any event, there was no way the case could have been thrown out at the magistrates' court. Whether it turns out murder or manslaughter, there was certainly a case to answer.'

'Is Mr Chalmers a reasonable sort of person?'

'He's not one of our locals. Has an office in Marylebone. I'd not come across him before, but he seemed all right. I think he was a bit overawed by his client, or rather by his client's father. He certainly hasn't given us any trouble to date.'

'Maybe I'll get in touch with him.'

'Good luck.'

'Thanks for telling me all you have.'

'You're welcome.'

At a quarter past five that evening, Richard presented himself at the offices of Chalmers & Co. He had phoned for an appointment and introduced himself as someone seeking urgent legal advice.

When he was shown into Mr Chalmers' office he was greeted with more than slight suspicion.

'Are you related to Mr Laurence Deegan who recently died?'

'I'm his younger son.'

'I see.' Mr Chalmers compressed his lips into a disapproving line. 'And you have come to see me professionally?' he asked sceptically.

Richard had the grace to look somewhat ashamed. 'Not really, but I wanted to talk to you privately and I thought you might baulk at seeing me if I said so on the telephone.'

'What makes you think I shan't now ask you to leave immediately? I don't like being made the victim of subterfuge.'

He was a tall, thin man with sandy hair and a narrow face. On the bridge of his nose rested a pair of gold-rimmed bi-focal spectacles, over the top of which fierce pale eyebrows sprouted like ragwort on a cliff face.

Despite his air of stiff reproof, Richard felt reasonably sure that he was not going to be asked to leave immediately. If only because Mr Chalmers was intrigued to learn the purpose of his visit.

'I apologise, Mr Chalmers. But it was very important that I should see you and I didn't want to risk being refused.'

'So the end justifies the means?'

'Isn't that frequently your experience?'

'Let's leave my experience out of it, Mr Deegan. Now that you have gained admittance by your deception, the least you can do is to tell me without waste of words why you wish to see me.'

'It's about my father's death and the brief you sent him in the case of Terence Edward-Jones.'

'One moment; am I right in believing that you yourself are a member of the Bar?'

'That's my brother, Norris. I'm a Detective Constable in the Special Branch.'

'Perhaps that explains your use of subterfuge in getting me to see you. I imagine you're well versed in the practice of such wiles.'

The tone was hectoring, but Richard reckoned he had to accept a certain amount of simmering annoyance on the part of the solicitor. Nobody likes being made to feel foolish, lawyers less than most.

'As I was saying, Mr Chalmers, my visit concerns my father's totally inexplicable death and the brief you sent him. Both events took place on the same afternoon.'

'And how am I expected to react to that?' he asked in the same frostily legal voice.

'Do you know anything to suggest that they might be linked?'

'I do not. And if I did, I certainly couldn't consider discussing a client's affairs with a third party. Indeed, I might say with a complete stranger.'

'Does it help if I say that I recently met Mr Edward-Jones? A meeting which took place at his instigation.'

Mr Chalmers raised one eyebrow off the top of his spectacles in apparent surprise.

'That still doesn't entitle me to discuss his affairs with you,' he said, though in a less frigid tone.

'Do you have any idea why he was so keen to have my father defend his son?'

The solicitor pursed his lips. 'Perhaps you should address that question to him.'

'My father's clerk told me what you wrote in your instructions to counsel. That Mr Edward-Jones was insistent that my father should be briefed and was determined to see his son acquitted.'

'The clerk had no right to disclose such matters to you.'

'He acted from the best possible motive.'

'Nothing can transcend the importance of complete confidentiality between a lawyer and his client.'

And I'm sure he really believes that, Richard reflected. To

77

Mr Chalmers, the small print of legal practice would be more compelling than the Ten Commandments.

'Look, Mr Chalmers, let me try and get you to see it from my angle. My father, who appeared not to have a serious care in the world, suddenly kills himself. There has to be an explanation. It's not medical, so what is it? Obviously something critical confronted him and caused him to take his decision. I'm reasonably satisfied that it was connected with one of two cases in which he was about to defend. One of them was R. *v.* Terence Edward-Jones. You had never briefed my father before, but you did on this occasion at the insistence of Mr Edward-Jones senior. The clerk had scarcely told my father of the arrival of the brief in Chambers when he began to behave out of character and, a few hours later, is found dead with his wrists slashed.' He paused and, fixing the solicitor with an earnest look, went on, 'If you were in my shoes, wouldn't you want to find out why? Wouldn't you be determined to solve the mystery? Wouldn't you? And if you're tempted to say that such enquiries are better left to the police, I would remind you that once suicide is established and there are no accessories involved, the police lose all further interest, there being no crime for them to investigate.'

A small superior smile caused the solicitor's mouth to unfreeze momentarily. 'Has it not occurred to you, Mr Deegan, that if your father had wanted you and others to know why he was taking his life, he could very easily have left a note of explanation? Has that possibility not entered your head?'

Richard managed to hide his irritation, not only at the question, but at the tone in which it was asked.

'Yes, it has occurred to me and other people, beside yourself, have also made sure I hadn't overlooked it, but I still feel that I must find out why he acted as he did.'

Mr Chalmers made a pinnacle of his finger-tips and studied the effect with judicial gravity.

'It is true,' he said, as if about to make an important announcement, 'that the brief was sent to your father on the express instructions of Mr Edward-Jones senior. I had not previously briefed Mr Deegan, though I've long recognised him as a leading figure at the Bar. But we solicitors are apt to be conservative in our use of counsel and stick with those we know. It was for that

78

reason only that I had not had any professional dealings with your father.'

Richard nodded impatiently. 'Did Mr Edward-Jones tell you why he wanted my father to defend his son?'

'I think, Mr Deegan, that we shall be crossing the Rubicon if I answer that question. Nevertheless, seeing that the answer is in the negative, I'm prepared to let you have it.'

'You never asked him?'

'As you've met Mr Edward-Jones, you will realise that he is not a man who can readily be pressed into giving information. I naturally did enquire why he was so eager to have your father in the case and he told me it was because he had followed his career in the newspapers and had no doubt he was the right person to defend his son.'

'Did he mention that he knew my father?'

'Are you asking a question or telling me something?' the solicitor said, once more hoisting one of his fearsome eyebrows. 'If it's a question, the answer is no, but I trust I can rely on you never to reveal the details of our present conversation now that the Rubicon has quite definitely been crossed.'

'I shan't tell a soul,' Richard said equably. He wondered what lay beneath the legal carapace of Mr Chalmers' persona. Was there a man with ordinary human likes and dislikes? Or was he stuffed with the dust from his own law books?

'And did they know each other?' Mr Chalmers asked keenly, breaking in on his thoughts.

'Yes, they did their national service together after the war.'

'I was not aware of that.'

'One confidence deserves another,' Richard remarked with a faint smile. 'One final question, if I may. Is Mr Edward-Jones a client of long standing?'

'I'd never met him before. As we say in the profession, he came in off the street. And before you ask a supplementary final question, I will tell you that he's a friend of one of my clients and that was how he came to select my firm. His own solicitors, he told me, don't handle major criminal work.'

'If that's so, wouldn't you have expected them to put him in touch with a firm that did, rather than leave him to his own devices?'

Mr Chalmers gave a delicate shrug. 'You'll hardly expect me to comment on that.'

As he walked away from the solicitor's office, Richard reviewed his day's progress. When he had been talking to Detective Superintendent Alcester he felt certain that the explanation of his father's death lay hidden somewhere in the Kulka case. After all, it was the brief in that case which his father had abruptly and apparently irrationally rejected. But now he found the pendulum of his thoughts swinging determinedly back toward Tom Edward-Jones. His talks with Norris, Detective Sergeant Angelo and, most recently, Mr Chalmers had served only to enlarge the question mark that hung over their past relationship. A relationship of which Edward-Jones spoke ambiguously and of which his father had never spoken at all.

CHAPTER XI

Norris Deegan was worried. In fact, very worried. There was nothing particularly unusual about this as he had always had a worrying disposition. As a small boy taking his first faltering steps he had worn an anxious frown. Now, twenty-five years later, his face was seldom without one. Worried frowns, peevish frowns, indignant frowns and (most frequent of all) disapproving frowns succeeded one another like rain clouds scudding across a grey sky.

He had never found it easy to get on with other people and this included his parents. Moreover, he had, as a child, always been aware of his resentment of his adopted brother, who had been all the things he was not. Friendly, cheerful and affectionate. He was thankful when at last he was grown up and able to make his own choices in life, though not even marriage and his own home succeeded in erasing his frowns or diminishing his worries. In truth, as soon as one worry was removed it was promptly replaced by another. His nature didn't permit a vacuum.

His current major worry was his brother and, in particular, Richard's determination to probe their father's death. He had already indicated his disapproval, but realised this wouldn't be sufficient to deter Richard. He now fell to pondering what further action he could take to halt him before it was too late, for there was no doubt in his mind that the risks were horrific. He didn't under-estimate his brother's tenacity which made them all the greater, nor did he hide from himself that his main motivation was self-interest. It was the effect on his own career that concerned him most. If Richard burrowed away indiscriminately, the consequent revelations could put paid to his prospects at the Bar. They might not do much good to Richard's prospects either, but that was far less serious to a young police officer than to a budding barrister. And, anyway, there'd be poetic justice in Richard undermining his own career. What was intolerable was that he should be putting his brother's at risk! It was so intolerable that he must somehow be stopped.

Thus ran Norris' thoughts as he left Chambers that evening to go home, though he had been thinking of little else since Richard's telephone call earlier in the day when he wanted to know whether their father had ever talked to him about his time in the army. It was obvious that he was off on some trail or other and, even if he couldn't be stopped in his tracks, it might at least be worth trying to deflect him.

Norris had little doubt that his father's army service was a false trail. And the reason he had little doubt was because he, Norris, knew why his father had taken his life. He was certain, moreover, that he was the only person who did know. Other misty figures might suspect, but *he knew.*

He could remember now the knock-out shock of discovering that his father was a member of a semi-underground political organisation which held extremist views. As so often happens, the discovery had been fortuitous, but its effect had been to throw him into a turmoil not long before he sat his Bar exams. He had told nobody and had also shrunk from confronting his father with his knowledge. It had happened only a few weeks before his marriage to Joanna and he had scarcely been able to wait to shake off what he regarded as the final ties of family life.

His father's rejection of the Kulka brief, followed almost immediately by his act of self-destruction, made sense to Norris in the light of his own secret knowledge.

He had, of course, sought to rationalise why his father had waited two weeks before telling Stanley to return the brief. He reckoned that, though he had not read it, he must have been aware of it ticking away like a time-bomb in his room. It was, however, only when Stanley fixed a consultation that he realised how close was the moment of detonation.

For, if Norris' deductions were correct his father would have been required to blow the case and ensure Kulka's conviction.

This would have been the nature of the pressure put on him by those with whom he had thrown in his lot. The threat of disclosure must have constantly hung over him, as it did over all who became embroiled with the Brotherhood of Racial Purity and demurred at its instructions. The National Front was pink and innocuous by comparison, according to one magazine article which Norris had read.

'Are you feeling all right?' Joanna asked anxiously when he arrived home.

'Yes, perfectly all right.'

'You look so white.'

'I always look white,' he said, as he came across and kissed the cheek she proffered.

'You're not going to work after dinner, are you?' she said, frowning at his brief-case.

'Only for about half an hour.'

'Because I've asked a couple from my office round for coffee. You've heard me mention Pam. She's married to a solicitor. I thought he might send you some briefs when he knows you.'

Norris put on his disapproving frown. 'I hope you didn't say that. It'd be most unethical.'

'Of course I didn't, but I suggest you ply him with our best brandy. There's still some left in that bottle my father gave us at Christmas.'

Joanna had recently changed jobs and now worked as personal assistant to a partner in a small public relations firm. She and Norris had been to dinner with her new boss and his wife, but the remainder of her colleagues were no more than names to him.

As things turned out, the evening was not a success. Norris was silent and preoccupied for much of the time and after the guests had left (early), Joanna took him to task.

'I know you're not the most sociable of people, but you hardly even tried this evening. I can only say that you let me down badly. I shall have to tell Pam in the morning that you weren't feeling well, otherwise she'll think I've married a moron.' Norris' silence stung her into further recrimination. 'You don't seem to realise that life hasn't been very pleasant for me since your father's death.'

83

'What's happened?'

'What's happened!' she echoed shrilly. 'It's not very nice having everybody know that one's father-in-law committed suicide and having to put up with funny looks and whispers behind one's back.'

'I'm sorry if that's happened.'

'It's not even as if I liked him very much,' she went on petulantly. 'Why should I have liked him when he tried to prevent us getting married? He never bothered to hide his feelings toward me.'

Norris stood with his arms hanging limply at his side, letting the verbal darts ping against him. When Joanna was in one of her waspish moods, he had learnt that it was better not to make any riposte as this only fuelled her further.

'Let's go to bed,' he said, when she had finally finished.

'You can go. I've still got the supper things to wash up,' she said sulkily. 'Anyway, I thought you had some work to do.'

'I'll get up early and do it in the morning. I'll give you a hand with the dishes.'

'Oh, Norris,' she exclaimed in a suddenly choked voice, 'I'm sorry. I didn't mean to be so beastly. I was upset. Tell me what's wrong; why you're so preoccupied?'

'It's the aftermath of father's death,' he said, gazing vacantly at the tray of dirty coffee cups. 'And Richard!'

'You mean, that silly idea of his of trying to find out why your father killed himself?'

Norris nodded. 'It's worse than silly.'

'Why not get your mother to speak to him?'

He gave a hollow laugh. 'She's much more likely to listen to him than to me. You know what she's like.'

He longed to confide in Joanna and tell her what he knew and of his fears. But, as so often in his life, he felt himself imprisoned within the lonely stockade his nature had erected.

It was a long time before he finally fell asleep as his mind turned over the various possibilities of thwarting Richard's intentions.

CHAPTER XII

It was two days later when Richard returned to Scotland Yard from a morning of keeping observation on a Palestinian student, who was believed to have terrorist connections, that he found the letter on his desk. It bore a first class stamp and was postmarked London, SW1. The envelope was type-written and had 'Personal' in the top left-hand corner. He knew that it would have been examined for booby-trapping before arriving on his desk and he slit the envelope without hesitation. A photograph fell out on to the floor. Before picking it up, he peered inside the envelope, which was empty. Apparently there was no covering letter.

He leaned over the side of his chair and stretched out his hand to retrieve the photograph. For several seconds he stared at it with a bewildered expression.

Whatever he had been expecting to see, it had not been a photograph of a cigarette case. But what immediately seized his attention were the engraved initials on the right-hand side of the case at the bottom. 'L.H.D.', which, as far as he was concerned, identified but one person. His father, Laurence Henry Deegan.

He looked at the reverse side of the photograph, but nothing was written there. It was just a photograph of a cigarette case bearing his father's initials which had been sent to him anonymously.

To the best of his knowledge, his father hadn't smoked for over ten years, apart from the occasional cigar on special occasions. But even when he had been a cigarette smoker, Richard couldn't recall his having possessed a case. And this was an expensive case, too, from its appearance. Probably solid silver and with the initials simply but tastefully engraved.

He picked up the photograph again and stared at it. Though it was perfectly clear in its detail, it lacked a professional patina. It could never have found its way into a jewellers' catalogue. The case was lying flat on a piece of black material which was crumpled round its edges and the camera had been held over it, but not directly above so that the perspective was slightly distorted. The initials L.H.D., however, were unmistakably clear.

He slipped the photograph back into the envelope, which he then placed in one of the cellophane wrappers he kept in his drawer. He would ask his mother about it when he called to see her that evening.

Fay Deegan was on her second drink when he arrived at the flat about half past six. Since her husband's death, she had been drinking more than usual. She was aware of the fact, but persuaded herself that it was purely a temporary phase which she could control if that became necessary.

'Hello, Mum.' Richard greeted her cheerfully when she opened the door. He noticed that she had a glass in her hand and decided he had better keep an eye on her to make sure she didn't overdo the booze. He had never before known her carry her glass with her when she went to open the door. He followed her into the living-room and went across to pour himself a beer, before joining her on the sofa.

'Why don't you go away for a bit, Mum? A change would do you good.'

'Go away where?'

'The south coast. Or if you feel more adventurous, what about Madeira or the Canary Isles? They'd be nice and warm at this time of year.'

'I don't like small islands. I'm not a beach person and I don't play bridge. And that only leaves drinking,' she said in what Richard thought was a faintly defiant tone.

'Why don't you go somewhere with Aunt Ruth? You could convalesce together; she from her operation and you from the traumas of the past two weeks.'

'Perhaps,' she said vaguely. 'In the meantime, you can pour me another drink, Richard.' She held out her empty glass. When he returned it to her refilled she said with forced brightness, 'And what's been happening since I last saw you?'

'It was only two days ago, Mum.'

'Yes, but have you found out anything yet?'

'Nothing worth mentioning. By the way did Dad ever possess a silver cigarette case?'

'Not to my knowledge. He virtually gave up smoking ten or twelve years ago. When we were first married he was a moderate smoker, but he always carried them in the packet. But why do you ask?'

'I came across a snapshot of a case with his initials on it and I just wondered if it had been his.'

He hoped his mother would accept this somewhat bland explanation and not ask any awkward questions.

'I expect there are quite a lot of people with the same initials,' she said in a tone of dying interest.

'Probably.'

By the time he had left three-quarters of an hour later, he had made up his mind to visit his grandmother. Grannie Deegan was now in her mid-eighties and lived with a companion near Bury St Edmunds. She had been over thirty when she married and had been widowed within five years. Richard visited her regularly and he decided that he and Sophie would drive up and see her that coming Sunday, provided she was well enough.

Maidie, the companion, opened the door of the bungalow in which they lived on the outskirts of the city.

'Come in, Richard, she's been looking forward to your visit ever since you phoned.' She gave Sophie a friendly smile.

'How is she, Maidie?'

'Apart from her sight, remarkably well considering.' This was Maidie's standard reply to all enquiries about the old lady's health. 'Don't forget, Richard, she's not been told how your father died.'

'No, I won't let anything slip out.'

Although his grandmother had, of course, been told of her son's death, it had been decided not to give her the exact circumstances. She knew he had died suddenly in Chambers and had been left to assume a heart attack. The deception was made possible by her inability to read the newspapers.

She was sitting in her usual high-back chair in the window when Richard and Sophie came into the room.

'Here they are,' Maidie called out, as she opened the door. 'I'll be in the kitchen if you want me.'

Richard went across and planted a kiss on her soft, smooth cheek. 'Hello, Grannie, I've brought Sophie with me. You remember her, don't you?'

The old lady continued holding his hand as she looked up into his face through the blue-tinted spectacles she always wore.

'Of course I remember her. I'm not completely ga-ga yet.' She peered past Richard without releasing his hand. 'How are you, Sophie?'

'I'm very well, thank you, Mrs Deegan,' Sophie replied, approaching the old lady on her other side. She bent over and kissed her lightly on the cheek.

'Sit on that chair, dear,' Grannie Deegan said, gesturing at one facing her across a small table on which a box of tissues and various pill bottles rested. 'You sit beside me here, Richard,' she went on, still clutching his hand. 'It's the first time I've seen you since your father's death,' she remarked in a matter-of-fact tone, confirming what her daughter-in-law had always said. Namely, that the very old often take death in their stride, even of near and dear ones. 'Of course, it's nice to die quickly and without any pain, but, even so, fifty is too young and I shall be minded to say so to the Almighty when I meet him.'

Richard gave Sophie a look of wry amusement.

'I suppose he'd been working too hard,' the old lady went on. 'People burn themselves out these days. Make sure you don't do that, Richard.' She gave his hand a quick squeeze.

'No danger of that in my job, Grannie.'

'No, I suppose you face other dangers. All these men of violence who infest our country. Why, Maidie was reading me something from the paper just recently about a girl of fifteen who shot her father and mother and sister because she was bored. The world's gone mad.'

'I don't think that happened in England, Grannie.'

'I don't remember, but that it could happen anywhere is

88

appalling. The trouble is that discipline has been undermined at every level of society.'

'I agree with that,' Richard said firmly. On the whole, he regarded his grandmother as being remarkably 'up-to-date', but it would have been unnatural if there wasn't some part of the scene around her which she deplored.

'Don't try and butter me up, Richard Deegan,' she said sharply, and immediately let out a merry laugh.

'But I do agree, Grannie,' he protested. 'Every policeman is aware of it. There's no longer any respect for authority, starting in the home and spreading through every aspect of life. When Sophie and I have children, they'll be strictly brought up, I promise you.'

'I didn't know you were married yet, Richard dear,' the old lady exclaimed in a startled voice. 'Why wasn't I told?'

'We're not, Grannie. I'm merely looking ahead.'

'Well, don't leave it too late! Not that I shall be able to come, but I should like to know you're married before I go. By the way, how's Norris?'

'He's well. Working hard to build a practice at the Bar.'

'He'll never do as well as his father. Hasn't got the brains. Funny the way you've always been much more one of the family than he is.'

'He's basically a shy person.'

'Shyness is often another word for selfishness.' Richard had always been aware that he was the favourite of her two grandsons, but had never sought to take advantage of it. 'And his wife, how's she? I can never remember her name.'

'Joanna. She's all right as far as I know.'

'You don't like her, do you?'

'I didn't say that, Grannie.'

'Your tone of voice said it for you.'

'I don't dislike her, though I admit she's not my favourite person. She's not very nice to Sophie.'

'Why not?'

'She seems to look down on her.'

'Then she's a fool. I hope you don't let it worry you, dear,' she said, looking in Sophie's direction.

'I don't. In any event, we don't see one another very often. It would worry me, however, if I thought it was coming between Richard and Norris, but it isn't as if they've ever been all that close as brothers.'

The old lady nodded vaguely. 'I hope you liked my son,' she said abruptly.

For a moment, Sophie looked non-plussed, unused to hearing her once future father-in-law so described. 'Oh yes, I did,' she said, as soon as she realised who was under discussion. 'He was always sweet to me.'

'I suppose I was lucky in a way,' the old lady mused. 'He never gave me any trouble. It wasn't easy for him growing up as an only child and without a father. He used to have to play a lot by himself which isn't good, particularly if a child has a secretive streak in his nature.'

'I never thought of Dad as being secretive,' Richard remarked.

'If he didn't want to tell you something, nothing would drag it out of him.' Then to Richard's startled ears she added, 'I often used to think he'd make a good spy. Nobody was better at keeping secrets.'

Richard drew a silent breath. The moment seemed to have arrived to broach the subject that was uppermost in his mind.

'He never talked about his time in the army, Grannie. Was that because he hated it?'

'I don't think he hated it. At least, his letters at the time didn't convey that impression. Rather the reverse, as I recall. Mind you, I think the young officers worked quite hard, but they used to play equally hard. Lots of parties in the mess and that sort of thing. I remember one of his friends telling me how drunk they used to get on Saturday nights. Laurence would never have told me that, of course, but this friend of his did.'

'Do you remember the name of the friend, Grannie?' Richard asked eagerly.

'It was Frank somebody, I think.'

'Not Tom somebody?'

'No, not Tom. I'm almost sure his first name was Frank. He spent a night at the house in Colchester where I was living. He and Laurence came back on leave together and he couldn't get home that day so he spent the night with us. He was a cheerful, freckled young man with carroty hair.'

'Do you remember where he lived, Grannie?'

'I believe he came from Shropshire. I recall his saying that his father owned a large farm.' She gave Richard's hand a convulsive tug as though it were a bell-rope. 'But why are you so interested in him?'

'Because it's a part of Dad's life that is something of a closed book and I'd like to meet someone who knew him in those days.'

'It's a long time ago. I don't even know if Frank's still alive; though he probably is as he was about the same age as Laurence.'

'Did you ever meet any of his other army friends?'

'No.'

'Do you happen to remember any of their names?'

'No. I never bother with the names of people I've not met. Anyway, your father often referred to them only by their first names.' A thoughtful expression came over her face. 'I do remember the colonel's name. He was Colonel Wheeler. He was later killed in Aden, poor man.'

'Did Dad talk to you about his national service later?'

She shook her head. 'He went straight from the army to Cambridge and then it was a question of making up for lost time. He loved Cambridge and his first introduction to the law. It occupied his mind to the exclusion of everything else.'

'Did he keep in touch with any of his army friends?'

'Not that I recall.'

'Not even with Frank somebody?'

'I think it was only the friendship of propinquity. It wasn't more than a superficial relationship.'

'Dad used to smoke in those days, didn't he?'

The old lady nodded. 'There wasn't all this fuss about smoking then. Most young men did. When he was commissioned as a second lieutenant, I gave him a silver cigarette case with his initials on it.'

Richard could hardly keep the note of excitement out of his voice when he spoke. 'Do you know what happened to it?'

'He lost it in Germany. I remember thinking, that's the last time I give him an expensive present. But, of course, it wasn't.' She paused. 'Young men don't carry cigarette cases these days, do they?'

91

'A few do. But most smokers just carry their cigarettes in the packet.'

'I used to enjoy an occasional cigarette, until the doctor advised me not to smoke because of my chest,' she observed wistfully. 'Thank goodness he hasn't tried to stop me drinking, which reminds me it's time we had one. Give Maidie a shout, Richard, otherwise she'll announce that lunch is ready and we shan't have time.' She released her grandson's hand and peered in Sophie's direction. 'You'll have a drink, won't you, dear?'

'I'd love a glass of sherry.'

'Good, so would I. Do you smoke? I ought to have asked before?'

'No. I tried it, but didn't like it. Richard doesn't either.'

'I thought he did.'

'He gave it up, too.'

The old lady smiled. 'All for the love of you,' she sang in a quavering voice.

Sophie laughed. 'I don't know about that, but I managed to persuade him he'd be fitter. The trouble is that most of his colleagues smoke, so he has to be extra strong-minded not to start again.'

'Fortunately he's well-endowed in that department,' Grannie Deegan remarked. 'Ah, I hear the drinks arriving.'

As soon as lunch was over, Maidie firmly led the old lady away for her rest and Richard and Sophie prepared to drive back to London.

It was as he was kissing his grandmother goodbye that she said suddenly, 'I remember that boy's name now. It was Frank Hare. I recall his saying that it was all right as a name, but he didn't like it to eat. Luckily I'd made a fish pie for supper.'

CHAPTER XIII

Richard was silent for the first twenty minutes of the drive home. Sophie could see he was deep in thought and didn't interrupt him. She was filled with contentment. Visiting Grannie Deegan had made her feel one of the family, which she liked; moreover, the sun had come out and there was the first real smell of spring in the air so that she inhaled deeply at the half-open window each time they passed a fresh meadow.

'Happy?' he asked abruptly, giving her a sidelong glance.

'Mmm. And your grannie's a darling.'

'I know. It's funny to think I used to find her quite fierce when I was small. But most old ladies become darlings if they live long enough. She's lucky having someone like Maidie to look after her.'

'How long has she been with her?'

'About ten years.'

'She remembered all about the cigarette case,' Sophie remarked after a pause.

Richard nodded. 'But it's still a mystery who sent me that photograph and why. That's what has been occupying my thoughts these past few miles.'

'Why didn't you show her the photograph?'

'Because she wouldn't have been able to tell it from a snapshot of Everest.'

'I was forgetting about her sight. She's so bright, she makes one forget.'

'I know. But supposing she had been able to see it, she'd have wanted to know how it came into my possession and who had taken it and heaven knows what else.' For the next half-minute he gave his attention to negotiating a busy crossroads. When they were safely over, he went on, 'What puzzles me is that if Dad lost his cigarette case in Germany, the photograph must have been taken thirty years ago.'

'If he lost it, the odds are that someone found it. It may even have been stolen from him. It could still be in someone's possession.'

'Tom Edward-Jones, for example.'

'Could be.'

'But why's he kept it all these years?'

'Blackmail.'

'Blackmail? I can't make sense out of that. How could my father be blackmailed over his own cigarette case?'

'I don't know.'

'Nor do I. And, anyway, why send me a photograph of it?' He became lost in brooding thought again. Suddenly his expression brightened. 'I've got a pal in the photographic section. I'll show it to him tomorrow. He'll be able to assess its age. It certainly doesn't look like thirty years old.'

'It could be a fresh print from an old negative.'

'Just what was passing through my mind, too. If it was Tom Edward-Jones who sent it, why? And if it wasn't him, who was it?'

'Are you going to try and find Frank Hare?'

'You bet I am. We'll have a look in the telephone directory when we get back to town.'

For several miles he had been driving almost mechanically; steering, braking and changing gear as reflex actions, but now he put his foot down hard on the accelerator and the car responded with its customary mixture of agitated sounds.

Sophie sighed. She had been hoping that they might dawdle back and perhaps even find an idyllic spot for a walk, but it was obviously not to be. Or so it seemed until Richard suddenly said, 'Shall we stop somewhere for half an hour? It's a heavenly afternoon and it seems a pity not to enjoy the countryside before we plunge back into grimy bricks and mortar.'

Sophie nodded happily and a few minutes later he turned off down a lane which wound ahead of them in the direction of a small lonely hill crowned by a copse. Half a mile farther on, the lane made a sudden kink to the right and a rutted track ran off half-left toward the hill. Richard turned up the track and parked.

It took them twenty minutes to reach the top, after a final steep clamber over tufted grass and loose stones.

'Worth it for the view,' he said, sitting down in the shade of a tree and gazing at the peaceful countryside that stretched before their eyes.

Sophie flopped down beside him, panting from the exertion. 'It's all so peaceful,' she said between gasps.

'More than you are, love! You're going in and out like a pair of ancient bellows. Here, lie back and rest your head in my lap.'

As she did so, he bent over her and gave her a long kiss.

In a later break between kissing her, he said, 'It may be very idyllic, but there's no getting away from the fact that it's bloody uncomfortable. I've got a stone digging into my right buttock and ants almost everywhere.'

'It's still worth it,' Sophie murmured, dreamily.

'It's all right for you, you have me as a mattress,' he said ruefully. After a pause he added, 'But I agree, it is worth it.' He ran a fingertip lightly round the contour of her mouth. 'Have you noticed the way everyone assumes we'll get married? Except, of course, Grannie who thought we already were. Well, why don't we start thinking about a date? After all, we can't disappoint everyone's expectations, can we?'

'Oh, Richard,' was all Sophie managed to say in a stifled voice.

'So what's your answer?'

'Yes.'

'You do realise that I'm formally proposing to you?' he said, his eyes shining brighter than any stars Sophie had ever seen. 'Because,' he went on, 'anything you say will be taken down in writing and may be given in evidence.' He peered into her face. 'Oh, lord, don't cry!'

'But I'm so happy,' she said, raising her head until their lips were within touching distance.

Ten minutes later they made their way back to the car, arms locked round one another's waists. On the return journey to

London, they made one further stop. At a pub to have a celebratory drink.

'Why should we feel so happy just because we've confirmed something we've long taken for granted?' he said, as they set off on the final lap of their journey home.

'Some girls don't realise what they're missing out on by skipping engagements and marriage and just shacking up with their boy-friends. They really don't.'

Richard threw her a quizzical look. 'We're not exactly a couple of old-fashioned virgins,' he said gently.

But he could see from her expression that nothing would spoil her illusion. And perhaps she was right and it wasn't an illusion at all. Casual shacking up was quite different from holy matrimony, even where a bit of its holiness had been forfeited before the event.

When they reached London, Richard drove straight to Scotland Yard. Leaving Sophie in the car, he dashed into the building. When he returned about ten minutes later, she could see that he was excited.

'Shropshire's full of Hares,' he said, adding with a note of triumph, 'but there's only one Frank Hare. What's more he lives on a farm and I have his telephone number.'

He thrust a piece of paper into Sophie's hand. On it he had scribbled, 'Frank Hare, Border Farm, telephone: Oschurch 3406.'

CHAPTER XIV

Fay Deegan had not been long awake when the telephone rang. It was later than she normally got up, but she had been sleeping badly since her husband's death and had been taking tablets prescribed by her doctor, which seemed to take effect just as the new day was beginning. In any event, she had no particular reason for getting up as early as she used to and had formed the habit of returning to bed with the newspaper and a cup of strong coffee.

She reached out for the receiver, imagining it to be Richard calling to report on his visit to Grannie Deegan the previous day.

'Is that Mrs Deegan?' an unknown male voice enquired.

'Yes.'

'I hope I haven't called too early, Mrs Deegan, but I wanted to make sure of catching you before you went out. My name's Bernard Powell . . .' He paused as if waiting for a reaction but when none was forthcoming, he went on, 'You won't know my name, Mrs Deegan, but I should like to come and see you at your convenience. Today if possible. Even this morning. May I do that?'

'What do you want to see me about, Mr Powell?'

'I'd sooner explain that when we meet. I'd prefer not to discuss it over the telephone.' In a sardonic tone, he added, 'I can assure you, however, that I shan't be trying to sell you a set of encyclopaedias or anything of that nature. It's a matter concerning your late husband.'

'What time do you wish to come?'

'Would half past ten be too early?'

She glanced at her bedside clock which showed nine fifteen. 'No, that would be all right. You know the address?'

His crisp 'yes' implied that he knew a good deal else besides.

Fay finished her coffee and got up. While she was having a shower, she wondered what she should wear for her visitor. He sounded like someone of consequence. His voice had been that of a person used to authority. It had also carried a note of clinical detachment, like an eminent surgeon who avoids any emotional involvement with the patient in whose vital organs he is hand-deep.

She decided on a plain charcoal grey dress, which would enable her to wear the rope of pearls Laurence had given her and augmented over the years of their marriage. It was the perfect dress for showing them off.

By the time she was ready, it was twenty minutes past ten. The bedroom would have to wait to be tidied until after he was gone. Closing the door firmly behind her, she went into the kitchen and prepared to make some fresh coffee. She had just switched on the electric percolator and set out two cups and saucers on a tray when the door bell rang.

Glancing up at the moon-faced clock on the kitchen wall, she saw that it was exactly half past ten.

She peered through the spy-hole of the door and could see a man standing back from it, but apparently staring straight at her. He was compactly built and looked about forty-five.

'I'm Bernard Powell,' he said, stepping forward as soon as she opened the door and dangling an identity card in a plastic holder for her to see. 'Convenient devices those,' he went on, gesturing toward the spy-hole. 'Important thing is to stand back so that you can be properly scrutinised.'

He was wearing a three quarter length dark blue top coat and a fur hat which Fay could see was genuine astrakan. He removed the hat as he stepped past her into the hall to reveal a head of well-groomed black hair with a long, straight parting on the left side.

'Shall I leave my things here?' he asked, taking off his coat and placing it with the hat on a chair.

'Would you like some coffee, Mr Powell?'

98

He sniffed the air. 'That would be very nice. There's no better smell, is there?'

'If you like to wait in the living-room, I'll fetch it.'

When she returned carrying the tray, he was standing with his back to the fireplace, hands clasped behind him. It had been one of Laurence's most favoured postures and she felt a sudden lump in her throat. How dare this mysterious stranger remind her so acutely of her husband! He wore such an air of self-assurance he could almost be doing it deliberately.

'Black or with cream?' she asked, quickly looking away as she put down the tray.

'Black, please. And no sugar. Have to watch my waistline.' She handed him his coffee. 'What a pleasant room you have! So light and airy and with a view of trees. Thank God for London's trees!'

'You mentioned you wanted to see me about my late husband, Mr Powell,' Fay said. She hadn't taken to her visitor sufficiently to indulge him in his small talk. 'Perhaps you'd start by telling me who you are.'

'But of course. My name you already know and I work in the Ministry of Defence.'

As he spoke, he fixed her with a hard stare.

'The Ministry of Defence?' Fay said in surprise.

'Yes. A large – one might say a *very* large – department which embraces a multitude of activities.'

'And where do you belong, Mr Powell?'

'I work in one of its less publicised sections. Perhaps I may leave it at that.' He paused while continuing to watch her intently. 'You appear surprised that my ministry should have an interest in your late husband.'

'I am.'

'Ah! Well, that answers one question.'

'Is it something to do with the Secrets Case he was about to defend in?'

'The Kulka case you mean? No, not specifically.'

'Then what?'

He replaced his coffee cup on the tray with exaggerated care, as though the move had required considerable thought.

'I know, Mrs Deegan, that your husband left no note explaining the circumstances of his untimely demise and that can only have added to your distress.'

'It most certainly has done.'

'And you've still no idea why he decided to take his life?'

'None. He didn't appear to have a care in the world.'

'So I gather.'

Fay felt another upsurge of irritation at her visitor's air of omniscience. Where had he gathered it from? And what business was it of his, anyway? He still hadn't explained that.

'It's only natural,' he went on, after flicking an invisible speck of dust off his sleeve, 'that you should be trying to find out what caused him to do it.' He met her gaze. 'I understand that and I'm personally sympathetic, but, nevertheless, it would be better if you desisted.' His tone had become suddenly uncompromising so that his words sounded more like an order than a suggestion.

'I don't think I understand,' Fay said, feeling the colour rise in her cheeks.

'What I'm saying, Mrs Deegan, is that it would be better not to probe the reasons for your husband's death. I hope that doesn't sound impertinent . . .'

'Oh, but it does,' she said in an even sharper tone than she intended. 'I'm afraid I don't take orders from the Ministry of Defence about the way in which I choose to conduct my life.'

'Please don't misunderstand me, Mrs Deegan. It's certainly not an order. That would be intolerably offensive. And, anyway, I have no authority to give orders of that sort. I assure you it's nothing more than a piece of friendly advice.'

'I don't even want your ministry's advice, Mr Powell,' she retorted.

He sucked in his lower lip and stared at her in his disconcertingly direct way.

'I've obviously upset you, Mrs Deegan and I'm sorry. That was the last thing I wanted to do. If I've been tactless, I apologise. Cut out the "if". I obviously have been tactless and I do apologise. How can I persuade you that my request is a reasonable one? Indeed, more than reasonable. Necessary. It really isn't a good idea to probe too deeply into his death.'

'Surely I must be the judge of that. But are you trying to tell me that you know why he killed himself?'

'No. I don't know any better than you.'

'Then why do you presume to tell me not to pursue the matter? If you don't know the answer, how can you say it ought not to be sought?'

'You're making it very difficult for me, Mrs Deegan.'

Fay shrugged. 'You can scarcely expect me to go down on one knee and apologise for that. After all, you invite yourself to my flat, tell me you're from the Ministry of Defence and proceed to tell me not to enquire into the circumstances of my husband's death.' She held up a hand when he was about to interrupt her. 'All right, advise, not tell, me, if you prefer, though it seems to amount to the same thing. I've listened to everything you've said, but am still left wondering by what right you offer me your advice, which I certainly haven't asked for. My husband mayn't have left a note explaining his death, but you haven't given me any satisfactory explanation of your visit.'

He ran a hand lightly across his head and down the back, where the hair had become slightly ruffled when he had removed his hat. Then he let out a heavy sigh.

'I hope it doesn't sound pompous, Mrs Deegan, if I say that my request is made in the national interest.'

Fay stared at him in astonishment.

'I had hoped,' he went on, 'to avoid mentioning that, but now that I have, I trust you will find it easier to accept the request.'

'You are asking me,' she said in a tone of incredulity, 'not to enquire into the background of my husband's death in the national interest?'

'Precisely.'

'But in what way is the national interest involved?'

'I'm afraid I'm not at liberty to answer that. I must ask you to accept that it is.'

'Are you saying that his death and the national interest are somehow connected? Because, if so, I just can't believe it.'

Her visitor gazed at her as if she was a particularly obtuse and obstinate pupil.

'I never said that. What I said was that it was not in the national interest to pursue enquiries into the circumstances of his death.'

'Isn't that the same thing?'

'No. As I've told you, Mrs Deegan, I've no more idea than

you have what prompted your husband to take his life. It's just that my department is very anxious there shouldn't be any wide-ranging enquiry into all the whys and wherefores.'

'Because of what might be discovered beneath some upturned stone?'

'Exactly.'

'Something which might have no connection with his death, but which you'd sooner remained hidden under its stone?' He gave a nod. 'You're implying that my husband had relations of some sort with your mysterious department.'

'If that's a question, I'm afraid I'm not prepared to answer it. I've already said more than I wished to, but I hope I've persuaded you in the end to drop your enquiries. It really would be the wiser course.' He fixed her with another of his authoritative stares. 'May I have your assurance to that effect?'

'There's only one snag, Mr Powell,' Fay said with a faint note of triumph. 'They're not my enquiries. They're my son's.'

He frowned. 'But surely at your request?'

'On the contrary, they're entirely his idea. He mayn't even tell me their outcome if he thinks I'd sooner not know.'

'I see.' Her visitor's tone was chilly and barely concealed his annoyance. 'Which of your sons is that?'

'I'm surprised you don't know! As a matter of fact, it's Richard.'

'Ah yes, the policeman!' He gave her a wisp of a smile as he got up to go. Fay followed him into the hall and watched him put on his coat and then carefully adjust the angle of his hat. She opened the front door when he was ready.

'Goodbye, Mrs Deegan,' he said in a tone that had all the friendliness of a spit in the eye from a llama.

CHAPTER XV

It was only when he had replaced the receiver after talking to his mother on the telephone that Richard realised he had not only failed to report on the visit to his grandmother, but had even omitted to mention that he and Sophie had become officially engaged. These had been the two purposes of his call, but his mother had given him no chance to speak before pouring forth an account of Bernard Powell's visit. Long before she had reached the end, his reasons for phoning her had been driven from his mind.

Nevertheless, he felt a certain sense of excitement after he had rung off. He was not a trained detective for nothing and here was yet a further clue to be investigated.

All he had discovered so far could be divided into two categories. In one, everything pointed to his father's death being connected with some sort of intelligence activity on which the Kulka case had had a cathartic effect. In the other, the indications were that it was linked to something in his past which had suddenly threatened to overwhelm him. In this second category came the refusal ever to talk about his time in the army, the curious intervention of Tom Edward-Jones and his enigmatic receipt of the photograph of his father's long lost cigarette case.

To date, the two sets of clues seemed irreconcilable, which made him feel like a circus performer riding round the ring balanced on two horses at the same time. All he could hope was that a third horse didn't suddenly appear.

On his way to work that morning, he had left the photograph

with his friend in the Yard's photographic section who had promised to let him know something by lunchtime.

With a sudden upsurge of impatience, he reached for his telephone.

'Eddie, it's Richard.'

'I was about to call you,' Eddie said in a faintly reproachful tone.

'I have to go out in a moment,' Richard lied, 'so I thought I'd better ring you. Any news?'

'Yes. It's a recent print all right. One can tell that from the paper.'

'How recent?'

'Not more than a few months old. Possibly made within a matter of days. I can't be more specific without detailed tests and even they mightn't be conclusive.'

'But it couldn't be thirty years old?'

'Absolutely not.'

'Thanks a lot, Eddie.'

'Hold on, I've not finished,' Eddie went on in his calm, equable tone. 'I've also formed a view about the negative from which the print was made.'

'Tell me.'

'It could easily be thirty years old. I've examined the photograph under a microscope and a number of tiny scratch marks are shown up. There's also evidence of a faint crease at one corner. All those marks came from the negative, which is far older than the print. Anyway, that's my view. There's also the suggestion of a fingerprint at one corner. It's very faint and can only be detected microscopically, but if you like to leave the photograph with me, I'll see if I can bring it up a bit clearer. It mayn't be possible to take the matter beyond that, but it's worth a try, I think.'

'Thanks again, Eddie. Incidentally, are you saying that the fingerprint is reproduced from the negative and hasn't been left by someone handling the photograph?'

'That's right, though there are fingerprints on that, too. Probably yours.'

'Probably.'

'But the other's the interesting one in the circumstances.'

'I agree.'

'I'll call you when I have something further to report, but it mayn't be for a few days so don't get impatient.'

It was one o'clock and though his tummy was giving the occasional protesting rumble (according to Sophie, it was more insistent than the cries of a starving baby), he decided it must wait a few further minutes before he went off to the canteen. It shouldn't take him long, he reckoned, to find out exactly who Bernard Powell was. That was an advantage of working in Special Branch. Such things could usually be discovered without arousing suspicion.

Half an hour later, as he stood in line waiting to be served, he wondered what on earth could be the interest Powell's section had in his father?

His discreetly made enquiries had elicited the information that Bernard Powell was second-in-command of a small, autonomous branch which kept a watchful eye on political organisations of an extremist nature. Not the better known ones, but those considered dangerous as well as cranky. It worked closely with the security service, but was housed separately, so that its existence was a well guarded secret. The Ministry of Defence provided a handy umbrella for its more overt activities, though, from what Richard could find out, it owed scant allegiance to that vast department.

As he watched the girl pile his plate with mashed potato, he felt more committed than ever to discovering what lay behind his father's death. On which side of the invisible fence had his loyalties lain? Richard prayed that it would prove to be the side of honour and patriotism, despite disturbing indications to the contrary.

As he carried his tray of food across to an empty table, he reflected that he had never before thought in such old-fashioned and emotive terms. For several seconds after he had sat down he stared at his plate, pondering the task he had set himself.

Though still determined to press on, he was now half-afraid of what he might discover.

As soon as he had finished his meal, he left the canteen. He was in no mood to linger and talk to a colleague over a second cup of coffee. He had a number of visits to make in the course of the afternoon, including one to Paddington Green Police Station where a Finnish seaman was in custody after having been arrested for being drunk and disorderly the previous night. When searched, he had been found to be in possession of a false British passport in the name of an Irishman suspected of gun-running. Special Branch had been notified in view of their interest in the man in whose name the passport was made out.

When Richard arrived at the police station and stated his business, the jailer grinned.

'You won't get any sense out of him today. He's got a hangover like the aftermath of a nuclear blast. I've never seen anyone as paralytic as he was when he was brought in last night. We couldn't even get him to court this morning. The doctor said he was the drunkest man he'd ever seen and that only a Finn could have survived.'

Richard wasn't sorry to have an excuse to defer his enquiry as he wanted to visit Chambers that evening and have a talk with Stanley. He put through a call to ascertain that the clerk was there and then set off for the Temple.

'Hi,' Mark, the junior clerk, said chirpily as he met Richard at the entrance to Chambers, 'I'm just off home, but you'll find Stanley and John in the clerks' room. Also Mr Hallick. Do you know him?'

'Only by name.'

'You've a treat in store,' Mark remarked, raising his eyebrows heavenwards.

Richard walked across to the open door of the clerks' room and paused uncertainly on the threshold.

George Hallick, the oldest member of Chambers, had his back to Richard and was addressing Stanley in a voice that was querulous and, at the same time, penetrating.

Stanley cast Richard a long-suffering smile and gently interrupted the harangue he was receiving.

'Have you met Richard Deegan, Mr Hallick?'

George Hallick turned round and gave Richard a suspicious stare. He was wearing the creaseless pin-stripe trousers and shiny black jacket that Richard had heard about. His hair was snow white and gave the appearance of having been trimmed in the dark with a pair of nail scissors. There were tufts of bristles on his face which his razor had missed.

'Ah, so you're Richard,' he said, holding out his hand. 'I've met your brother. Pity he didn't come into these Chambers. Never did find out why. I wrote to your mother. Hope she got my letter.'

'I'm sure she did, sir. She had so many, I'm afraid it'll take her a long time to answer them all.'

'You know it was my razor your father used?' George Hallick said, to Stanley's obvious embarrassment. Richard nodded and the elderly barrister went on, 'Not like him to be inconsiderate in that way. Shows he must have been in a state of turmoil when he did it. If you ask me, he'd pushed himself too hard. Sudden brainstorm. No earthly reason otherwise. Hard taskmaster the Bar. I've never allowed myself to become its slave.'

From what Richard had heard, it was the Bar which had shown no inclination to enslave George Hallick. He was one of its ancient failures who should have got out years before, but who lived from case to case, presenting a firm front of self-esteem.

'Your father led me a couple of times,' he now went on. 'I expect he told you about the cases. One was a divorce and the other was the defence of a dastardly fellow charged with the murder of his wife. The prosecution accepted a plea to manslaughter on the grounds of diminished responsibility and he got five years.'

'I think I remember my father mentioning the case,' Richard said politely, which was true. What his father had actually said was that he would sooner go into court without a junior than have George Hallick. 'I wouldn't mind if he did nothing at all,' he had remarked. 'But his unhelpful stage whispers and his talent for passing one the wrong document are severe tests of one's patience.' He had added that if charity began at home, leading George Hallick in a case was its highest form.

'Both interesting cases in their way,' Hallick said. 'We made a formidable team, your father and I. He with all his advocate's flair and I with my long experience at the Bar. Mind you, I'm not sorry I never took silk. I've much preferred life as a junior.'

Richard noticed Stanley staring steadfastedly at a spot on the floor. It was common knowledge in the Temple that George

Hallick had applied for silk on several occasions and been refused.

'Well, Mr Hallick, I'm afraid there's nothing for you tomorrow,' Stanley said in the intervening silence.

'Then I'll take a day off. My flat could do with a bit of a clean.' He turned back to Richard. 'I live alone and it's not easy to run a practice and a home, you know.'

He ambled out of the room, giving Richard a brief nod of farewell.

'Does he have much work?' Richard asked, after Stanley had closed the door and they had both sat down.

Stanley let out a heavy sigh. 'I have the greatest difficulty scraping together any for him. He's past it, but refuses to recognise the fact. There are one or two solicitors who know him and who, more out of charity than anything else, entrust him with small, unimportant cases, but that's about all. Poor old chap, I'm afraid he's become something of an embarrassment. However, that's not what you've come to talk about! How are your enquiries going?'

'I'm not sure.' He paused and meeting Stanley's gaze, went on, 'Were you aware of my father ever having any links with the security service or any of its offshoots?'

'Over the Kulka case, do you mean?'

'I meant generally.'

Stanley looked at him in surprise. 'No I wasn't. Why should he have had any such links?'

'Before I answer that, tell me whether you've had a visit from anyone in the security service about the Kulka case?'

'Someone did come here a few days after the brief had been delivered. Said he wanted to be sure that your father and I understood the importance of keeping the brief under lock and key. I told him that I'd already heard that from the police officer in charge of the case and that we were used to handling highly confidential papers in Chambers and that he need not doubt our discretion.'

'Did he see my father, too?'

'No. He wanted to, but Mr Deegan was out and I persuaded him it wasn't necessary. I got the impression it was a routine visit and he seemed quite happy with our security arrangements.'

'Do you happen to remember his name?'

'Brown. It suited him, too. An anonymous sort of name for an anonymous-looking person. Now tell me why you're asking these questions?'

After Richard had given him the gist of Bernard Powell's interview with his mother that morning, Stanley said, 'I'm completely mystified. I've no idea at all what this man Powell was getting at. Are you going to let his visit to your mother affect your enquiries?'

'No way. I'm more determined than ever to dig out the truth. I must go on, Stanley, I couldn't just drop everything now. And as for Mr Hallick saying Dad must have had a brainstorm, it's nonsense.'

'I agree, though I did think it the most likely explanation at first. Possibly because it was also the most comfortable explanation.'

'Was there ever anything to suggest that Dad was leading a double life?'

'Certainly not. I'm sure he wasn't.'

'And yet in a sense, he must have been. By which I mean that he had a secret life away from the one we all knew.'

'If so, it was certainly very well hidden. He never gave the slightest inkling of it.'

'Did you know that he attended receptions at the Czech Embassy?'

Stanley stared at him in astonishment. 'I most certainly didn't.'

'Well, he did. That's where he first met Mr Weinstock, the solicitor in the Kulka case.'

'You astound me.'

'And it rather looks as if that's the mere tip of the iceberg.'

'Are you sure you wish to go on, Richard?' Stanley asked in a worried tone. 'May it not be better to let sleeping dogs lie? I know I encouraged you, but in the light of what you've just told me, I'm doubtful about the wisdom of your continuing your enquiries.'

'Mr Justice Hensley thinks I should.'

'When did you speak to him?'

'A few days ago.'

'I wonder if he'd still be of that mind if you told him what you've just told me. It gives a different complexion to the whole affair.'

'I thought you were my ally, Stanley.'

'I am, but I have to think of the good name of Chambers. Moreover, supposing you uncover something to your father's discredit, would you want it blazoned abroad?'

'It wouldn't have to be. Nobody, but myself, need ever know.'

'Easier said than achieved.' Stanley let out a heartfelt sigh. 'Go and see Sir Sam again and be guided by what he says,' he said with a resigned air, He met Richard's stony gaze. 'I'm still on your side, Richard, but what you've told me today has made me afraid. Afraid of what you may uncover.'

Richard had arranged to return to Paddington Green Police Station at half past eight the next morning. By then, it was confidentially predicted, the Finn would have recovered his powers of communication. He reckoned that his visit ought not to last more than forty-five minutes which would give him time to get to the Law Courts and see Mr Justice Hensley before he went into Court.

A telephone call to the judge's home that evening elicited the information that he could come along any time after half past nine and the judge would be delighted to see him.

'It's very good of you to give me more of your time, Uncle Sam,' he said, after finding his way to the now familiar room.

'I told you I'd be available if you wanted my advice and I meant it. So what's been happening?'

It took Richard twenty minutes to bring the judge up to date on events.

'So you see, it's really because of Stanley I've come. He's worried about what I may unearth, but I'm sure he'll go along with whatever you advise.'

'He's afraid you're opening a Pandora's box and won't be able to get the lid back on again, is that it?'

'Yes.'

'What's your mother's feeling?'

'I think she was so incensed by the Ministry of Defence man's visit, she'd do anything to cock a snook at him, which, of course, I'll be doing on her behalf if I continue.'

110

'Cocking snooks is a form of self-indulgence and is sometimes better suppressed,' Mr Justice Hensley remarked with a judicial air.

'So you agree with Stanley then?'

'I didn't say that, though I understand his anxiety up to a point. He obviously has to think of Chambers. Anything that gave Chambers a bad name could affect the livelihood of its members.'

'I don't see how anything my father got up to can affect others if they weren't involved in any way.'

'In a fair and just world, it wouldn't. But guilt by association has become a modish concept. Odious, of course, but, nevertheless, something that has to be faced. If it emerged, for example, that your father had for years been engaged in some utterly nefarious practice, it could easily shake the confidence of some of the solicitors who send work to those Chambers and cause them to look around elsewhere. That's what Stanley is anxious about.'

Richard bit his lip in a worried manner, but remained silent. It seemed that his allies were deserting him one by one.

'You've told me so much I never knew and would never even have guessed at that I'd like to take time to think about it, Richard. I know judges are trained to deliver judgments as soon as the advocates sit down, but there are occasions when one needs time to reflect and this is one of them. How are you placed this evening?'

'I'm not doing anything special.'

'Come along to my club at six o'clock, and we'll find a quiet corner and have a drink. Meanwhile, I shall think hard about what you've told me.'

There was a knock on the door and the judge's clerk looked in.

'I'll be ready in a couple of minutes, Stephen,' Mr Justice Hensley called out, jumping up from his chair and walking across to where his robe was hanging. 'When I was at the Bar, I used to get very cross with judges who seemed to make a habit of arriving late on the Bench. I swore then that, should I ever become one, I would never keep the court waiting.' He glanced at himself in the mirror over the mantelpiece and pulled his wig slightly forward. Satisfied with the result, he made for the door.

'Can you find your way out all right, Richard? See you at six o'clock.'

When Richard arrived in his room at Scotland yard, Detective Constable Tinkler, who was on the phone, glanced up, rolling his eyes in desperation. He took the receiver from his ear and held it out toward Richard who could hear a female talking in a heavy foreign accent.

'I'm very sorry, Mrs Pariades,' Tinkler broke in, 'but I can't help you. It's nothing to do with this branch. You'll have to sort it out with the Home Office Immigration Department . . . Yes, they're still at the same number I gave you two days ago . . . No, not at all . . . goodbye, Mrs Pariades.'

He replaced the receiver and flopped back in his chair with arms flung limply over the sides.

'If I ever discover who gave that woman my number, I'll strangle him or her.'

'Haven't you asked her?'

'Of course I've bloody asked her, but you try getting a simple answer out of Mrs Pariades. All you get is the story of her life all over again.'

'What's her problem?'

'Verbal diarrhoea, flat feet and falling hair. If I could cast spells, she'd have a few more. She has a niece, or it may be a third cousin twice removed, who is having trouble over the renewal of her passport and someone told her, Mrs Pariades that is, that Special Branch had a wand they could wave in such cases and that it was kept in the drawer of a certain Detective Constable Patrick Tinkler. Anyway, you needn't look so pleased with yourself, Richard, the Commander was trying to get you shortly before you came in.'

'Commander Cucksey?'

'Who else!'

'Is he expecting me to call him back?'

'I asked that and the answer was no. He was about to go out and would get hold of you later.'

'I wonder what he wants. Moreover, I wasn't feeling pleased with myself.'

'You looked it.'

'I was merely being polite to you.'

'That'll be the day!' The phone on D.C. Tinkler's desk rang. 'If that's Mrs Pariades, you'd better stand by with a fire bucket.' A few seconds later, however, he replaced the receiver and grinned. 'They've arrested that dodgy Indian I was telling you about. The one with a different passport for each day of the week. He's at Heathrow, which is where I'm off to.'

It was about an hour later that Richard received a summons to Commander Cucksey's presence. He was a tall, thin man with a deceptively languid appearance and a faintly bored tone of voice. He was neither popular nor unpopular with his subordinates. He certainly never sought to be the first and gave the impression of being quite unbothered if he was the second.

Richard, who had had very little personal contact with him in the course of his work (their difference in rank saw to that), regarded him with a degree of ambivalence.

Commander Cucksey was on the telephone when Richard knocked and opened the door of his room. He motioned him to take a seat. While Richard waited for the conversation to end, he glanced about him without displaying too obvious a curiosity. On a side table close to his chair were three photographs. One was of an unsmiling woman posing at the piano, whom he assumed to be Mrs Cucksey. Next to it was a smaller photograph of a solemn bespectacled boy of about fourteen. He had hair worn in a schoolboy fringe and his face was quite expressionless. Richard reckoned that the trauma of being formally photographed was probably responsible for his lifeless air. The third photograph had been taken outside Buckingham Palace after an investiture. Commander Cucksey was wearing a top hat which made him look like a chimney stack. He was displaying the OBE he had just received for the benefit of the photographer. His wife was still unsmiling (and no wonder, thought Richard, with a hat like the one she was wearing) and their son was looking bored. Indeed, on the evidence of the photographs and the man sitting on the other side of the desk, it was difficult to envisage the Cuckseys as a happy family group.

The Commander finished his conversation and made a note on the pad at his side. For a few seconds, he studied what he had written down, then slowly he lifted his head and looked across at Richard.

'I understand, Deegan, that you've been making your own enquiries into your father's death.' The tone was neither hostile nor friendly, just flat and to the point. Commander Cucksey had never had a reputation for beating about the bush.

'Yes, sir. It was so inexplicable that I felt I must try and find out why he killed himself.'

'Hmm! Is this something you've undertaken entirely on your own initiative?'

'Yes, though my mother knows what I'm doing.'

Richard had already divined that he was going to be warned to keep off. Obviously Bernard Powell had lost no time in bringing pressure to bear. And of course he was much more vulnerable to pressure than his mother would be.

'So you're really only motivated by curiosity, eh?'

'I wouldn't describe it that way myself, sir,' Richard replied, stung by the crudity of the question. 'I think any normal son would react as I have. I happened to be devoted to my father and his death came as a shattering shock. I have to know what drove him to do it.'

'Is that your brother's view, too?'

Richard bit his lip. He felt certain that Commander Cucksey already knew Norris' view or he wouldn't have accompanied the question with such an aggressive look.

'No, sir, it's not. But then my brother wasn't as close to my father as I was.'

'These enquiries you're making, they must take up quite a lot of your time.'

'My own time, sir. Not official time.'

'You weren't in until half past ten this morning. What delayed you?'

'I was at Paddington Green Station at half past eight interviewing a man detained there, sir,' Richard retorted quickly, hoping Commander Cucksey wouldn't ask for a more detailed timetable of his movements.

'It's generally undesirable that any police officer should undertake a private investigation. Even in his own time. It can give rise to misunderstandings, if not complications.' The Commander stared pensively at his unsmiling family on the side table. 'And, of course, the position is even more delicate where a Special

114

Branch officer is concerned. Indeed, the misunderstandings and complications can be quickly multiplied. You follow me?'

'Yes, sir. You want me to drop my enquiries.'

'Not me personally, Deegan, but there are those who have their reasons for hoping you will desist.'

'Mr Bernard Powell, I take it, sir. He called on my mother yesterday morning.'

'He was only doing his duty.'

'I'd like to be quite clear, sir. Are you giving me advice or is it an order?'

Commander Cucksey made a small grimace. 'I'm dropping you a friendly hint which I think you'd be well advised to take.' He paused and looked once more at his family photographs as if they were the fount of all wisdom in his room. 'After all, you have your career ahead of you. It'd be a pity to do anything to jeopardise that.' He raised a hand as if to ward off a missile. 'No, that's not blackmail or anything like it, but you've been in the police long enough to know that it's best to keep in step. There's plenty of scope for initiative without ignoring the guidelines by which we all have to live.'

'Does it affect your advice, sir, if I say that my father's death may have nothing whatsoever to do with Mr Powell and his outfit – whatever their interest is. It's quite possible that it relates to something that happened thirty years ago.'

'I think it would still be better if you stopped probing the circumstances,' Commander Cucksey said after a few seconds reflection. 'After all, while looking for one thing, you may stumble across something wholly unexpected. That's the danger.'

'Can you give me any idea what Mr Powell's interest is in my father?'

'That's easily answered. I don't know because he didn't tell me. All he did say was that he was alarmed at the prospect of the shock waves your enquiries might set up and that it wasn't in the national interest for you to pursue them.'

'It's always easy to invoke the national interest,' Richard said a trifle bitterly. 'It'd be better if Mr Powell took me or my mother into his confidence.'

'I can't speak for your mother, but what I have said should be sufficient for you as a Special Branch officer.' His tone was severe. 'I should now like to have your assurance that you will drop your investigation.'

Richard looked at him aghast. 'Assurance, sir?'

'Your oral assurance.'

'May I have time to consider my position, sir?'

'It shouldn't be necessary, but you can have till tomorrow morning.'

'And if I feel unable to give you an assurance, sir?'

'Let's not anticipate events, Deegan!'

As he returned to his room, Richard bleakly reviewed the possibilities. If he stood his ground, he might be transferred out of Special Branch on the grounds that he had shown himself unfit to be entrusted with all the confidential information with which it was daily concerned. Or he might be kept on and assigned to duties which kept him out of London. A sort of punishment posting to the equivalent of Siberia, save that it wouldn't be expressed as crudely as that.

It was in a mood of gloom and despair that he approached Mr Justice Hensley's club at six o'clock that evening. The porter on the door told him the judge was in the bar and seemed surprised when Richard enquired where it was located.

'I gathered you were an old friend of his lordship's,' he said, with a sniff.

'I am, but I've not been to this club before.'

'Oh well, it's where it's always been. Up the main staircase and you'll find it facing you at the top. You can't miss it, it'll be the only room with noise coming out.'

In fact, there were only four people in the bar and if one of them had not had a particularly loud laugh, no sound at all would have greeted Richard's arrival.

Mr Justice Hensley was at one end of the bar talking in a desultory manner to a fellow member, but he detached himself as soon as he saw Richard in the doorway.

'What'll you drink, Richard?'

'Do they serve beer?'

'Bottled, not draught.'

'That'll be fine.'

'Brown ale? Lager?' He glanced at the barman who was waiting for their order. 'What other beer do we have?'

116

'Lager and brown ale, sir.'

'Lager, please,' Richard said, amused by his host's wry grimace.

'Arthur's been our barman since time began, but I've never yet been able to decide whether he's deaf or dim-witted or just a bit fly,' Mr Justice Hensley remarked as he returned with the drinks and led the way to a small settee in one corner of the room. 'He's certainly all there on some things, such as what he considers an equitable distribution of the staff Christmas fund.' They sat down and he went on, 'I didn't ask you this morning, Richard, but how are your superiors likely to react if they learn of your unofficial enquiries?'

Richard gave a mirthless laugh. 'If you *had* asked me this morning, Uncle Sam, I'd probably have said I didn't think they'd object, provided there was no conflict of interest with my work. But now the answer is that they do object, and I've been told to lay off.'

'Hmm! I thought that might happen in view of the man Powell's visit to your mother. You're much more vulnerable to pressure than she is. I suppose he's already spoken to your superiors?'

Richard nodded and related the gist of his interview with Commander Cucksey. When he had finished, he said, 'Does that affect the advice you were going to give me?'

'What I had been going to say was that you should follow the dictates of your conscience. If that sounds like the sort of thing the Delphic oracle served up, let me explain. It can be rather dangerous advice if given to the wrong person as some people have somewhat misshapen consciences. Others, of course, have public consciences, of which I'm always suspicious. It's only because I believe you to have an honest, straightforward conscience, Richard, that I was proposing to tell you to be guided by it. You obviously wish to continue your enquiries and I'm sure you can be relied on to be discreet and circumspect over what you find out – and that if you do uncover something detrimental to your father's memory, you'll keep it to yourself. That, of course, may be easier said than done. However, every course of action in life entails some risk and provided you're aware of the hazards (and I know you are) they seem to me to fall within

117

the acceptable category.' He reached for his drink and swallowed a mouthful of Scotch before going on. 'But what has happened today has to be taken into consideration. Your superiors are not going to like it if you ignore their wishes and, as they've hinted to you, your career prospects could be jeopardised. It adds up to an additional risk of a rather different sort.'

'I'm not sure, Uncle Sam, that I would want to stay in a job where my personal freedom of action is restrained by official considerations.'

'I wouldn't be too hasty to adopt that line, though I sympathise with your reaction. But most of us have to accept restrictions on our so-called freedoms. Have you ever thought of the restraint a judge has to accept? He has to be careful where he does his drinking. He can't make any public utterances out of court that might reflect on his judicial integrity. He has to be especially careful not to become involved in any traffic accident, even as an innocent party. We're all subject to inhibitions of one sort or another on account of our work and we accept them because we recognise that they're for the benefit of a well-organised society.'

'But that's just it, Uncle Sam,' Richard broke in vehemently, 'I don't accept that telling me to lay off enquiring into my father's death is any business of society.'

'You've been told it's in the national interest you should cease.'

'Told, yes. But why should I accept that without being given an explanation.'

'As an officer of the Special Branch, you should be in a better position than most to accept it. After all, your work must frequently involve you in matters of national interest where the security of the State is concerned.'

'But Dad never did anything to harm his country,' Richard exclaimed. 'It's the daftest suggestion anyone could make.'

Mr Justice Hensley eyed him thoughtfully for a few seconds. 'I don't imagine the mysterious Mr Powell visited your mother on a sudden whim or just for fun.'

'No, of course he didn't. But there's obviously been some gigantic mistake.' Observing his host's dubious expression, Richard went on, 'Believe me, Uncle Sam, mistakes do happen even in those well regulated corridors. The members of the intelligence services are as capable of monumental cock-ups as anyone else. They generally manage to suppress theirs, however, on the grounds that it wouldn't be in the public interest to allow them to be known.'

Mr Justice Hensley gave a small laugh. 'I have no reason to doubt what you've just said. But if it's what has happened in the case of your father, they're still not going to thank you for burrowing away. The contrary, in fact. They're going to thwart you with every weapon at their disposal, fair or foul. And I imagine they have a formidable arsenal of both types.'

Richard nodded ruefully. 'Little did I ever expect to be at the barrel end.'

'And so what are you going to do?'

'If I go ahead, are you intending to wash your hands of me?'

'Good gracious, no. I'm sorry if I've given you that impression.'

'You haven't, Uncle Sam, but it would be understandable in the circumstances.'

'My services will remain at your disposal, Richard. My shoulder will be available for weeping on, though I hope it won't be needed for that. Have you thought what you're going to tell your Commander tomorrow?'

Richard gave a small squirm. 'I suppose you can't think of a form of words, Uncle Sam? Something that'll satisfy him without completely binding me.'

'The spirit of any agreement is usually more important than the words,' Mr Justice Hensley remarked drily. 'But you could give him an assurance that you won't do anything to embarrass your department. That would enable you to continue investigating your other line of enquiry without colliding with Mr Powell's interests. Provided you go about it discreetly, I don't see that your superiors are likely to find out.' Mr Justice Hensley glanced at his watch. 'Let's have another drink and then I must go. Seeing your mother tonight?'

'No, I'm going out with Sophie. Incidentally, we're now officially engaged.'

'I'm delighted to hear it. She sounds a nice girl. I know your mother likes her.'

'Dad did, too.'

As he made his way to the bar, Mr Justice Hensley reflected on Richard's devotion to his late father. He hoped that future events would do nothing to undermine it. While he waited to be served he wondered whether his advice had been sound. On the whole he thought he had struck the correct balance of view. But, of course, there was no gainsaying the influence of his own considerable curiosity about his friend's death.

Personally, he had always held the secret belief that Laurence Deegan might one day reveal a flawed character. He would seem to have been proved right.

CHAPTER XVI

Sophie had been delayed on her way home that evening. She had a ten minute walk from the bus stop which was about half a mile from her house and was hurrying as she wanted to have a bath and change before Richard called for her.

She had reached the end of her road and had just stepped on to the zebra crossing when there was a screech of tyres and a car cut round the corner. If she had not leapt back quickly, she would have been hurled to the ground or possibly carried forward on the car's bonnet. Either way, serious injury or death seemed certain in view of the car's speed.

She leaned, shaking, against the crossing bollard as the car roared away up the road, accelerating all the while. There had been no question of taking its number, it had been going much too fast for that. Moreover, her impression had been of a dirt-encrusted vehicle with a mud-covered rear number plate. It was a sports car, fairly old and red in colour, she thought and that was the sum of her impressions in the twilight.

Her legs felt ready to buckle as she started to walk along the pavement. She had only a hundred and fifty yards to go, but she had never been so relieved to see her own front door.

The experience itself had been bad enough, but it had been the fleeting glimpse of the driver's expression that had really unnerved her. From it, she knew that it had been a deliberate attempt to scare her.

As she let herself into the house, her youngest sister called out from the front room, but Sophie sank down on to the hall chair and rested her head against the wall. She closed her eyes, but opened them quickly when she heard Katie get up from the table where she was doing her homework.

'Why are you sitting there?' Katie asked, staring at her from the doorway.

'I suddenly came over a bit giddy, that's all. I'll be all right in a moment.'

'Will you help me with my homework?'

'I've got to change. Richard's coming for me.'

The corners of Katie's mouth turned down abruptly. 'You could still help me. I can change in two minutes.'

Sophie sighed. 'Where's Daddy?'

'He's gone next door to help Mr Oxley repair his T.V. He said he'd be back in about an hour, but you know Daddy once he starts fiddling with T.V. sets.'

'Where's Jean?'

'It's her night for choir practice. I don't know why they keep her in the choir as she can't sing at all. I expect the choirmaster has a crush on her.'

Sophie smiled. Katie had never been one for mincing her words.

'So you see, you've got to help me,' Katie went on. 'There's nobody else. But you're the best anyway. Daddy's all right on maths, but terrible on English. He doesn't even know what a gerund is.'

'What is today's homework?'

'Ugh! French and geography, I hate them both. Who cares whether it's *le plume* or *la plume*?'

'The French do.'

'It won't help me become a ballet dancer.'

'You'll never get to ballet school if you go on eating sweets the way you do. Your teeth'll fall out and you'll become as fat as Mrs Oxley.'

'I'm going on a diet tomorrow.'

'I wouldn't mind a penny for every time you've said that.'

Katie sighed. Though she had put on some weight, she was still far from being fat. But Sophie knew she picked at crisps and sweets when there was nobody around to stop her.

'I'm going upstairs to have a bath and change. I'll help you with your homework when I come down. If Richard arrives first you can ask him.'

'When's he going to buy you an engagement ring?' Katie asked cheerfully, as she turned back into the room.

'We're going to choose one at the weekend.'

'I shall have diamonds and emeralds in mine.'

'Any husband of yours is going to need a gold mine to support you.'

Before Katie had time to comment, the telephone rang. Sophie thought it was probably her father calling to find out if she was back and what her plans for the evening were.

She lifted the receiver and gave her number as she had been trained to do at her secretarial course.

'Tell your boy-friend to stop poking his nose where it's not wanted. Otherwise one of you may get hurt.'

There was an abrupt click as the receiver at the other end was replaced. Sophie put out a hand to steady herself and took a deep breath. The voice had been tough and uncompromising and had matched the expression on the car driver's face.

Thank goodness Katie had returned to her homework and Sophie could flee upstairs.

'Who was it?' Katie called out, as Sophie passed the sitting-room door.

'It was a wrong number.'

'How do you know?'

'The person at the other end realised it as soon as I lifted the receiver.'

'Was it a man?'

'Yes.'

'What did he say?'

'He just said, sorry.'

'Did he make heavy breathing noises?'

'No. Now get on with your homework or nobody will help you.'

It was with considerable relief that Sophie reached the bath-room and locked herself in. She turned on the taps and then had to hold on to the towel rail as she began to shake violently.

By the time she came downstairs, Richard had arrived. Far

from helping Katie with her homework, he was drawing her pictures of all sizes of hippopotami, which was one of his party pieces.

He jumped up as Sophie came in and went across to kiss her, watched by a dispassionate Katie.

'How are you feeling, darling? You look a bit frail.'

'She came over giddy when she arrived home,' Katie observed.

'I'm fine now,' Sophie said in a none too convincing tone.

'Shall we go then?'

'You can't go yet. You've got to help me with my homework,' Katie broke in indignantly.

'We'll have to wait till Daddy comes in. He's next door. He shouldn't be long. We can't leave Katie alone.'

'Why not?'

'You're not old enough.'

'I'm not a baby any more.'

'Tell Daddy, not me.'

About twenty minutes later, Mr Piper arrived back.

'Sorry if I've held you up, but it took longer than I expected,' he said. 'I take it you are going out?'

'Sophie's not well,' Katie said in a sly voice. 'She fainted when she came in.'

'I did not,' Sophie retorted. 'I just felt a bit dizzy. I'm perfectly all right now. Your trouble, Katie Piper, is that you're not only getting fat, you're also a little mischief maker.'

Katie grinned. 'Who's going to help me with my homework?'

'I will,' her father said firmly. 'Now sit down and get on with it.'

'I've done all the bits I can.'

Richard seized Sophie's hand and led her toward the door. 'Good night, Mr Piper. Good night, Katie.'

'Aren't you going to kiss me. After all, I am going to be your sister-in-law.'

Richard kissed her on the cheek and was amused to see her blush. Though whether with pleasure or embarrassment he wasn't sure.

'Are you certain there's not something wrong?' he asked anxiously when he and Sophie had got into his car. 'You don't look yourself and all this talk of fainting and feeling dizzy when you arrived home.'

As Sophie told him everything that had happened, his expression became more and more grim.

'Bastard!' he muttered angrily. 'Trying to get at me through you.'

'But who could it have been, Richard?'

'My guess would be it was an emissary of Tom Edward-Jones. It sounds the sort of crude tactic he'd engage in. He'd be just the type to believe he can frighten people into doing what he wants. The intelligence services may employ all manner of dirty tricks, but this doesn't bear their hallmark.' He shot her a worried look. 'Is there any chance at all that you might recognise the driver again?' Sophie shook her head. 'Or remember the registration number of the car?' She shook her head again. 'Are you sure that not even a couple of letters or numerals impressed themselves on your sub-conscious? Make your mind a blank and concentrate on the rear of the car as it sped away from you.'

'It's no good, Richard. All I know is that it was a small sports car and that it must have been dirty because I could only just see the tail lights.'

Richard sighed heavily. 'It must have been Tom Edward-Jones,' he murmured thoughtfully. 'There's no one else.'

'But what about the driver and the man who phoned?'

'Probably the same person. A young thug hired for the job.' After a pause he said, 'I think it'd be best if you left home for a bit. You could go and stay with my mother. She has acres of room and it'd only be for a short time.'

'I can't, Richard. Daddy needs me at home to help run the house. And what could I tell him without causing him alarm?'

'Then I'll have to come and pick you up every morning and drive you home in the evening.'

'It's not necessary, Richard. Forewarned is forearmed and from now on I'll be very careful how I cross streets and who I stand next to at bus stops.'

'I'm still not happy.'

'It's better than worrying Daddy and the rest of the family. Anyway, nothing further may happen.'

Richard wished he could feel equally sanguine, particularly as he had in mind a further probing of what he now regarded as the Edward-Jones connection. If he was careful, however, there was no reason why Tom Edward-Jones should find out anything at all. Perhaps the answer was to let him think he had ceased investigating his father's death. And the most obvious way of achieving that was to tell him so.

As they drew up outside the bistro where they often ate, he leaned over and kissed her.

'Don't get out till I tell you,' he said.

He came round to her side of the car and glanced quickly up and down the street before opening her door. He gave the bistro an equally careful scrutiny before they went in and found a table.

Before he went to bed that night, he sat down and wrote a letter.

Dear Mr Edward-Jones, (it ran)

Just a line to thank you for inviting me to drinks at the Croesus Club. It was interesting to meet someone who had known Dad before I was ever a gleam in anyone's eye. As to my enquiries into his death, I have received so much advice similar to yours that I have now reconsidered the whole thing. Perhaps it is better to let matters rest and not attempt to discover what happened. In any event, my enquiries were taking up too much of my time and so I've decided to drop them and leave the mystery of his death unsolved. Maybe time will provide an answer. Meanwhile, thank you again for your hospitality.

Yours sincerely
Richard Deegan

126

CHAPTER XVII

Fay Deegan had felt pleased when Sam Hensley telephoned and invited himself round for a drink at her flat. He had written her a long, understanding letter after Laurence's death, in which he had said he looked forward to seeing her when she had had time to become adjusted to life again. She had seen him at the funeral, but only for the briefest of words.

She had suggested he should come early as she was expecting Norris and Joanna for supper that evening, they having also proposed themselves.

'Hello, Fay.' Sam Hensley greeted her with a warm smile when she opened the door. 'I hope I'm not early. I'm afraid it's not yet six o'clock.'

'It's lovely to see you, Sam. You could never be too early in my home.'

He took off his coat and handed it to her as she stood waiting with a hanger in her hand. As they entered the living-room, she gestured in the direction of the tray of drinks.

'Help yourself, Sam. The Scotch is in the decanter.'

'What about you?'

'I poured myself one just before you came,' she said with a guilty laugh. 'I always need extra fortification when Norris and Joanna are coming.'

'You're not too fond of her, are you?'

'I've nothing against her. It's just . . .'

'That you find little in her favour, either?'

'I suppose that's about it. But she's fond of Norris – at least, I think she is – and he of her, so what else matters?'

Sam Hensley refrained from the obvious comment and said, 'There must be something wrong with the girl if neither you nor Laurence took to her.'

'I'm afraid he made his feelings rather obvious. And there was all that business when he tried to get them to put off their marriage. It left a sour legacy. Actually, as I'm sure you know, what he disapproved of was Norris getting married before he'd qualified. But Joanna chose to take it as disapproval of herself as his future wife.'

'She may have had some reason for so doing.'

'I suppose she did,' Fay remarked with a small grimace.

'However, more important, how are you?'

'Some days I feel fine; others I have a great black cloud hanging over me.'

'That's hardly surprising. You've undergone the mental equivalent of major surgery. It takes time to recover from the shock. Why don't you go away for a while? A complete change of scene can work wonders.'

'That's what Richard was saying to me the other evening.'

He peered at her thoughtfully over the top of his glass which he had raised to his lips.

'I don't know whether he's told you, but we've seen each other once or twice recently.'

'Yes, he mentioned that he'd been to see you.'

'About his enquiries into the background of Laurence's death.'

Fay gave an abstracted nod. 'I'm glad he sought your advice,' she said vaguely.

'You're content that he should do so? Probe the reasons for Laurence's death, I mean?'

She gave a slight shrug and peered into her glass as if it held answers for her. 'He's promised not to tell me anything he thinks I'd sooner not know. I'm sure I can trust him.'

'I'm sure you can. But it's not really the point. Or not the whole point.' She looked at him and blinked stupidly. 'Is there any risk of Richard finding out something to his own detriment?'

Her mouth opened and closed like a fish's. 'What do you mean, Sam?'

'Does Richard know who his real mother and father are?' he

128

asked, feeling that he was back in his role as an advocate, examining a difficult witness.

She shook her head and stared again into the depths of her glass. 'I've never told him. Not the woman's name, that is. He didn't wish to know.'

'You say the woman's name, but what about his father?'

'We never knew his name.'

'I probably have no business to be asking these questions, but my excuse is that I wouldn't want Richard to uncover details of his birth which are better kept hidden. At the moment, he's like a young retriever following up every scent he finds and it occurred to me that he might suddenly go after that particular scent without knowing where it might lead him.'

'He's never met his mother and neither have I. I've no idea where she lives or even if she is still alive. She parted with Richard when he was six weeks old.'

'But you know who she was?'

'She was a young girl who worked for Laurence's aunt up in Derbyshire. She was only eighteen at the time, a healthy country girl who had the misfortune to become pregnant by the first man who seduced her.'

'Who was he?'

'A boy from a neighbouring village, I understand. He was killed in a motor-cycle accident before Richard was born.'

'I assume his name never appeared on the birth certificate?'

'No. Only the mother's.'

'May I ask what it was?'

Fay furrowed her brow for a moment.

'I know her last name was Smith,' she said slowly. 'Was it Emily Smith? No, I remember now, it was Eileen. Eileen Smith.'

'Eileen Smith of Derbyshire twenty-five years ago,' he said in a reflective tone. 'I suppose she might still have relatives living up there?'

'I can't tell you.'

'What about Laurence's aunt?'

'She died five or six years ago and the property has been sold.'

'I see.'

What Fay Deegan had told him confirmed something that had been lodged at the back of his mind since the early days of

Laurence Deegan's tenancy in Chambers. It had been an oblique comment of Laurence's which had caused Sam Hensley to suspect that he, Laurence, might be the father of the baby they were then about to adopt.

If this were so, he could only assume that Fay had never had any inkling of the fact. Her story of the unknown young father conveniently killed in a motor-cycle accident had come out quite naturally and without any sign of embarrassment. Nevertheless, if she knew that Laurence was Richard's natural father, he'd have expected her to confide in him and say so. Weighing up the evidence with judicial care, he decided that if this was a case he was trying in court, his findings would be, first, that Laurence was Richard's natural father and secondly, that Fay was totally unaware of the fact. It seemed to him significant that the baby had been born to a girl who worked for Laurence's aunt.

As if to further confirm the conclusion he had just reached, Fay said, 'In some ways, I think Laurence was fonder of Aunt Hetty than he was of his own mother. She was never married and she always treated him as a favourite nephew.'

'Used he to visit her often?'

'Usually about twice a year, but when he was a young man he was always going up there to stay. She had a lovely old house on the edge of the Dales. The only thing was it was falling apart and needed tens of thousands spending on it by the time she died.'

'What age was she?'

'She must have been in her early eighties. I know she was several years older than Grannie Deegan. Incidentally, did Richard tell you he'd been up to Suffolk to see his grandmother last Sunday?'

'No.'

'He's much better than Norris about visiting her.'

'He's a naturally kind and thoughtful young man,' Sam Hensley observed. He was thinking, too, that the bond between Richard and his father was entirely explained if Laurence was his natural parent, even though Richard himself remained ignorant of the fact. The question was what would be his reaction should he ever find out? The odds against his doing so were formidable. It was extremely unlikely that he would ever be able

130

to trace Eileen Smith after all these years, even assuming he started nosing in that direction.

Though it was still possible that this aspect of Laurence Deegan's past had suddenly risen up in menacing form, it seemed less likely than Sam Hensley had once feared and he certainly felt happier now than when he had arrived.

He drained his glass and giving his hostess a cheerful smile said, 'May I get myself another drink, Fay?'

'Of course. And you can fetch me one, too.' As he carried the two empty tumblers across the room, she went on, 'I wonder if I shall ever adjust to widowhood as well as you have to life since Mary's death.'

'I've had longer to get used to being alone than you have. It'll be seven years in June.'

'You've never thought of getting married again?'

'I might have if the right woman had popped up at the right moment. But I doubt if I ever shall now. I've become used to living alone and the older one gets the more one becomes set in one's ways. I'll be sixty-seven next birthday.'

'That's not old.'

'Not for a judge, perhaps,' he said with a laugh, as he returned with their drinks.

'Why don't you stay and have supper, Sam?' she said on an impulse.

'That's kind of you, Fay, but I'm dining at my club tonight. I've promised to meet someone there.'

'At least stay and say hello to Norris and his wife.'

'I'd like to, provided they're not too late arriving.'

'I must leave you for a few minutes while I go and attend to something in the kitchen.'

He was glancing at a magazine when she came back into the room and she addressed his back.

'While I've been out of the room, I've been thinking about all the questions you asked me. Perhaps I may put one to you. Do you think *you* know why Laurence killed himself?'

He turned his head and staied at her in surprise.

'I've no idea, Fay. No idea at all. I'm sorry if I gave you that impression. It would have been thoughtless to say the least.'

131

'I just wondered, as you seemed to be following a train of thought.'

'I admit that I was. I didn't want him to discover anything about his origins that might unsettle him. But you've put my mind at rest on that score.'

She nodded and went on, 'Laurence would have told me if Eileen Smith had made herself suddenly known again. And, in any event, I can't see any possible connection between her and his death.'

'Good!' he said, as if that finally closed the matter. 'You probably won't be too upset if his death remains an unsolved mystery.'

'I think it'll be better if it does. The truth is often more hurtful than not. That's why I've asked Richard not to tell me anything I wouldn't wish to hear.'

'You almost sound as if you have your own theory,' he remarked.

She came across to her chair and sat down on the edge, nervously revolving her wedding ring on her finger.

'Theory?' she said, as though savouring the word. 'No, I haven't any theories. I've merely been compelled to face an unpalatable conclusion, namely that Laurence was suddenly confronted by something which made death seem preferable to life. Something I knew nothing about and which quite clearly he didn't wish anyone to know about.' She gave Sam Hensley a small bitter smile. 'I doubt whether you can call that a theory.'

'Something out of his past are you suggesting?'

'Or out of his present. I've no idea which and I prefer not to speculate. But it surely sticks out a mile that it can't be anything to his credit. Fortunately, I've always been a good ostrich. I'm adept at sticking my head in the sand and not seeing what I don't want to see. That's what I've been doing ever since his death. Of course, there've been times when I've had to pull it out, such as this evening for example, but I quickly bury it again.' She met Sam Hensley's concerned gaze. 'Do you blame me? Surely it is a case of ignorance being preferable to knowledge. Maybe it really is bliss in comparison. Who knows? In the same way that we're better off not knowing in advance the appointed day of our death, so I'm happier not knowing why Laurence killed himself.

132

If it's nothing to be ashamed of, Richard will tell me. That is, if he ever digs deep enough to discover the truth.' She paused for several seconds before going on. 'I had the press on the telephone several times just after it happened asking questions and making insinuations. One particular reporter refused to believe I didn't know why he'd done it. He kept on suggesting there must be either a sexual scandal or a financial one as the background. I suppose those would have been the most interesting to his readers. In the end, I used to put down the receiver as soon as I recognised his voice.'

Sam Hensley made a sympathetic sound. 'I'd no idea, Fay . . . Richard never mentioned it . . . I'm so sorry to think you had to put up with that sort of thing.'

'I realised it wouldn't last and it didn't. That's why I never told Richard or Norris. Richard would have been furious and might have taken some hot-headed action, so it was better he shouldn't know.' She let out a small sigh. 'I suspect that Norris would merely have told me that it was to be expected and the press was only doing its duty.'

'I know how relentless they can be in search of a so-called human drama story. Relentless and often pitiless as well.'

There was a buzz at the front door and Fay got up. 'That'll be Norris and Joanna now.'

While she was out of the room, Sam Hensley finished his drink. He wished now that he hadn't agreed to stay.

'Good evening, judge,' Norris said as he entered the room. 'You know Joanna, I think.'

'Good evening, Sir Samuel,' Joanna murmured, giving him a limp handshake.

'I've got a case waiting to be listed,' Norris went on. 'I'm hoping it may come in front of you.'

'We're so thick on the ground these days that the odds must be against. In any event, I shall be out on circuit most of next term.'

'Do you enjoy that?' Fay said, as she resumed her seat.

'I wouldn't want to be out of London all the time, but I quite enjoy six or eight weeks of being on the road. Of course, a lot depends on the time of year and which towns you visit. I'm off to Chester and North Wales which couldn't be pleasanter in the early summer.'

'I get a certain amount of work at Chelmsford,' Norris remarked importantly.

'Which means he can get there and back in the day,' Joanna put in. 'I don't like him being away at nights,' she added in a faintly proprietorial tone.

Mr Justice Hensley cast her an ironic glance, but said nothing. A few minutes later he got up and made his farewells.

'I'd like another drink,' Fay said, after he had gone. 'What about you, Joanna?'

But her daughter-in-law primly shook her head. She was the sort of girl who could make a thimble of sherry last half the night.

'You'll have another, Norris?' his mother said hopefully.

'Yes, I will,' he said in a tone that was suddenly grim. When he returned with the drinks, he said bleakly, 'This may be as good a moment as any, mother, to talk about Richard.'

'What about him?' Fay asked defensively.

'This stupid investigation of his. Surely, you're not in favour of it?'

'It's no use being angry with me, Norris, it's his investigation, not mine.'

'I'm not angry with anyone,' he said crossly. 'But can't you have a word with him and tell him to stop?'

'He already knows my view and, anyway, it's a matter for him.'

'That's just what it isn't. If he continues, we could all feel the effects. Look, Mother,' he went on, in a tone of heavily strained patience, 'surely you must realise what the risks are. I don't want to say anything to upset you, but surely you must realise that the reason Father killed himself must relate to something fairly murky in which he had become involved. If whatever it is should ever become public knowledge, it's not going to be pleasant for you and it could easily harm my career at the Bar.'

'You've said nothing I haven't already thought about, Norris. But I'm sure we can rely on Richard not to reveal anything which might be to your father's discredit.'

Norris let out an exasperated snort. 'I'm not saying he'd do it on purpose, but cats can jump out of bags before you know what's happened. The odds are, he'll have no control over events if he goes on burrowing away like a sow after truffles.'

'So what do you want me to do?'

'Tell him to lay off and concentrate on the job he's paid to do. Joanna feels as strongly about it as I do.' Joanna gave a solemn nod, as her husband went on, 'It's not fair on us or on you. I know Richard's always been a bit of a shining knight, but that doesn't give him the right to go against all our wishes. I'm sure you don't really want him to continue his foolish enquiries, Mother. It's no good my saying anything further to him, but he'd listen to you if you told him firmly to stop what he's doing.' He let out a small mirthless laugh. 'But you'd better not invoke me, just ask him to stop for your sake. You can say that you've been thinking again and that's your view. That you're worried about what may emerge and the effect it could have on your health, as well as on Father's reputation. Even Richard won't resist you if you pitch along that line.'

'I think I smell something burning in the kitchen,' Fay said, jumping up and hurrying from the room.

Norris stared after her with a look of despair. 'Have I got through to her?' he said.

'You can never tell with your mother,' Joanna replied tartly.

'I was in time to save our steak and kidney pie,' Fay said as she came back into the room. 'We can eat any time you're ready.'

'I'm sorry, Mother, but I refuse to be brushed aside by a steak and kidney pie,' Norris said. 'Will you or won't you speak to Richard? Because if you won't, I shall have to do something myself.'

'I'll think about it,' Fay said vaguely as she led the way to the dining-room.

Norris and Joanna exchanged ill-humoured glances as they followed her out of the room.

CHAPTER XVIII

Tom Edward-Jones always arrived in his office shortly after eight o'clock and was annoyed when he had to wait for others to clock in at a later hour.

On this occasion, the object of his annoyance was Mr Chalmers, who, he learnt from his secretary, would not be in until a few minutes after half past nine, almost as if he was determined to assert his prerogative to arrive after the rest of his staff.

A further source of irritation was the failure of his morning mail to appear. His secretary said there had been a hold-up in its delivery and he had despatched her to the sorting room to wait for it. He was accordingly not to know of Richard's letter to him when he did eventually speak to the solicitor.

Mr Chalmers, for his part, disliked receiving telephone calls almost before he had had time to take off his hat and coat and he had not been pleased to be informed on his arrival that Mr Edward-Jones had been trying to call him and would be doing so again shortly.

He had barely sat down at his desk when his phone rang and a cool voice asked him to hold the line as Mr Edward-Jones wished to speak to him.

'Mr Chalmers?'

'Yes. Good morning.'

'I thought you were going to fix up a meeting with this new counsel who'll be defending my son.'

'Mr Fullerton, you mean.'

'Have you been in touch with him?'

'I sent him the brief a few days ago. I doubt whether he'll have

136

read it yet. Counsel are not given to reading briefs too far in advance. That is, unless there's a special reason.'

'There is.'

'I'm not sure I'm with you, Mr Edward-Jones.'

'The special reason is that I'm the person paying the piper and I want a meeting. Anyway, why has it taken so long to send him the brief? You got it back from Deegan's Chambers over a week ago.'

'I had to redraft part of my instructions,' Mr Chalmers said in a frosty tone.

'Well, can you phone him and say I want to come and see him within the next couple of days?'

'I'll speak to his clerk . . .'

'Forget his clerk. Speak to the man himself!'

'I'm sorry, Mr Edward-Jones, but protocol has to be observed. It's the barrister's clerk who fixes conferences and consultations.'

'What's the difference?'

'Junior barristers hold conferences, but with a silk you have a consultation.'

'Well, get on to the clerk and say I want an immediate consultation. I went to see Terry in Brixton prison yesterday evening and the boy's feeling very low.'

Mr Chalmers' eyebrows, which had spent much of the last few minutes jutting out over the top of his spectacles like porcupine quills, now assumed a less militant look and came to rest on top of his spectacles.

'There was something else I wanted to say,' Tom Edward-Jones went on without waiting for any response. 'Has Deegan's son been in touch with you?'

The bluntness of the question took the solicitor aback, so that for once in his life he sounded flustered.

'Er . . . yes, I . . . er . . . believe he did come to see me.'

'You believe he did. You know damn well he did. What did he want?'

'I'm afraid I can't discuss other people's business,' Mr Chalmers said with a partial recovery of dignity.

'As long as you didn't discuss my business with him!'

'I resent your tone.'

'Come off it, Mr Chalmers, we're both grown men, there's no

need to pull lawyer's rank on me. I suppose he told you he was making his own enquiries into his father's death?'

'I think he did say something to that effect.'

'Did he ask questions about why my son's case had gone to his father?'

'Mr Edward-Jones, I hope I have made it clear to you that I do not discuss my clients' business with other people. You may rest assured that I broke no confidences when I saw young Deegan. I may add that he arrived here without having told me in advance the reason for his visit. If I had known, I would not have given him an appointment. As it was, I left him in no doubt that I did not welcome his visit.'

'I'm glad to hear it, because I wouldn't like to think that you gave him any sort of encouragement to continue his enquiries.'

'I didn't, though I'm not clear why you should feel concerned. I'm sure you have no need to be.'

'I hope not,' Tom Edward-Jones said in a steely tone. 'I don't like being worried unnecessarily and I'm liable to over-react. Well, I'll expect to hear from you later in the day about the consultation you're going to fix up with Mr Fullington.'

'Fullerton.'

'Never mind his name, I hope he's as good as you say.'

For several seconds after his caller had rung off, Mr Chalmers sat staring ahead of him with a furious expression. His eyebrows bristled with hostility. It was a long time since he had a client he so disliked. It was also, however, a long time since he had had one with such a ready cheque book.

Though he had been affronted by the call, he found that his curiosity had also been aroused. With a lawyer's care, he now took mental stock of the situation *vis à vis* his formidable client.

Surprise number one had been his insistence that Laurence Deegan be briefed to defend his son. Normally, clients accepted their solicitors' advice on the choice of counsel, at most they might express a preference. But Edward-Jones had been adamant that nobody other than Deegan should be briefed. Then had come the silk's mysterious suicide on the very day the brief was delivered. And coupled with that was Richard Deegan's visit.

After Laurence Deegan's death, Edward-Jones had left the selection of a new defending counsel entirely to his solicitor. He ad certainly insisted that he must be the best available and had repeated that money was no object. But Deegan's name appeared to be the only one he knew at the Bar and he hadn't even bothered to remember that of the new one who had been briefed.

As Mr Chalmers mentally surveyed these facts, he became more and more pensive. Eventually, he reached the somewhat sombre conclusion that the less he knew the better. There was obviously a potent background of some sort, but instinct warned him that it was probably one more treacherous than an uncharted minefield. On the whole, it was wiser to stay within the confines of his client's instructions and charge him every penny he could.

He emerged from his reverie and reached for his telephone. He supposed he had better call Mr Fullerton's clerk and seek to arrange an early consultation. He would stress the importance of their client and the clerk, recognising the euphemism, would know that importance and wealth were synonymous in the context.

CHAPTER XIX

The next few days passed off quietly, if uneasily, as far as Richard was concerned. He assumed that Tom Edward-Jones had received his letter and accepted it at face value. He had not received any response, but had scarcely expected to.

He had given his assurance to Commander Cucksey that he would make no further enquiries which could possibly embarrass Bernard Powell's outfit. The Commander had accepted the assurance in thin-lipped silence and had dismissed him with a nod, which had left Richard wondering who was deceiving whom. What he did quickly discover was a fresh load of work on his desk which was clearly designed to keep him so busy that he had no time for anything else.

At Friday lunchtime, he dashed out to his bank and withdrew £200 from his savings.

The next morning, he and Sophie went and bought the engagement ring. Her father had a friend in the trade who offered them a substantial discount, with the result that not only was Sophie delighted with her choice, but Richard had money left over.

After they had lunch together, he drove her home and set off immediately for Shropshire. He reckoned he should reach Oschurch in three to four hours, depending on the traffic and the behaviour of his car.

A telephone call to the local police had brought the information that Major Hare still lived at Border Farm. He was crippled with arthritis and seldom went far afield, the sergeant at Oschurch police station had told Richard. He lived with his wife and a married couple who looked after the house and garden. The

arm was run by a married son who lived in a house which his
ather had built for him as a wedding present.

Richard's intention was to stop the night at a pub in the
neighbourhood, from where he would phone Border Farm intro-
ducing himself and mentioning that he happened to be passing
through the district and felt it would be nice to say 'hello' as his
father had often talked about his old army friend, Frank Hare.

He realised that, for a host of unforeseeable reasons, his
expedition might end in a debacle. But that was a risk he had to
take. Sophie had agreed he would be better off on his own and
had waved him goodbye with her engagement ring prominently
displayed.

It was six o'clock when he arrived at Oschurch and looked
in at The Farmer's Haven. He asked the landlord's wife, who
showed him to his room, how far Border Farm was from the
village and was told it was two and a half miles to the west. He
gathered that Major Hare was a well-known and popular figure
in the district and that he could often be found in the Haven
before his arthritis restricted his mobility.

'Poor man, he really has suffered,' she said. 'He's had opera-
tions, but they don't seem to have helped all that much.'

'Is he permanently in a wheelchair?' Richard enquired.

'No, he has those elbow crutches, but it's painful to watch him
walk. And yet he's so cheerful with it. Mrs Hare's a lovely person,
too.'

Encouraged by this information, Richard decided to telephone
immediately. A woman's voice answered.

'Is that Mrs Hare?'

'No, who wants her?'

'My name's Richard Deegan, but it won't mean anything to
her. My father used to be in the army with Major Hare.'

There was no reply, but he could tell from the sound that the
receiver had been put down on a table. It seemed he was left
waiting an age and he was bracing himself for a rebuff when he
heard the receiver being picked up again.

'Mrs Hare speaking,' a pleasant voice said. 'Mr Deakin, is
it?'

'No, Deegan. Richard Deegan. My father was Laurence
Deegan, the Q.C. He did his national service in Germany with

your husband and often used to talk about him. I happen to be motoring through the area and wondered if it would be possible to call on you?'

'Where are you speaking from, Mr Deegan?'

'I'm stopping the night at the Farmer's Haven in Oschurch.'

'Are you leaving early in the morning?'

'About lunchtime.'

'Then why don't you come here for a drink around twelve?'

'I should like that very much.'

'Ted, the landlord of the Haven, will give you directions. It's only ten minutes by car and that includes half a mile of unmade-up road.'

'I look forward to meeting you and your husband, Mrs Hare. It's very kind of you to invite me. By the way, I ought to mention that my father died recently.'

'Yes, we read about it in the paper,' she said in a brisk yet compassionate tone. 'We'll expect you at twelve then.'

After an excellent meal cooked by Freda, the landlord's wife, he retired to the public bar where he spent the evening listening to the regulars talking and joining in only when invited to do so. At closing time he helped Ted and Freda clean up the bar and wash the glasses.

He had already discovered that he was the only guest stopping the night and that two was the maximum.

'We don't really mind if the rooms are not taken,' Ted explained. 'In fact, we'd probably have shut them but for a few regular customers who pleaded with us not to. Sales reps mostly. You'd think they'd prefer one of those places where they can have posh bathrooms and colour T.V., but they seem to like coming back here. I suppose it makes a change. But you're the first guest we've had on a Saturday night since last summer.'

'I can understand their returning if you feed them the way you did me. The places with posh bathrooms and colour T.V. often serve plastic food.'

'That's one thing we don't do, surrounded as we are by farms. Last time the wife and I were down in London, I don't think we were served a single fresh bit of food the whole three days we were there. It was all tinned or frozen. Looked all right, but had no more taste than coloured cardboard.'

142

After the clearing-up was finished, Ted invited Richard to join him in a nightcap, Freda having gone up to bed.

'We always clear up before we retire for the night,' he said, looking around with a satisfied air. 'Can't bear facing mess first thing in the morning.' He raised his glass. 'Well, cheers. You'll like the Hares, they're a grand couple.'

'How long have they lived at Border Farm?'

'Frank Hare was born there. The only time he's been away was when he was in the army.'

'I take it he must have stayed on after his national service.'

'That's right. Took a short-term commission and rose to dizzy major.' He gave a good-natured laugh. 'Funny the way some like to hang on to their military rank, not that I think it'd worry Frank Hare to be addressed as plain mister. He's a man without any side at all. But major he became and major we call him.'

It was nearly midnight when Richard went up to bed, but he fell asleep within a couple of minutes and didn't wake up until a shaft of sunlight caught him full in the face. His watch told him it was nine o'clock.

As he had it in mind to drive back to London immediately he left the Hares, he was happy to accept Freda's offer of a cooked breakfast. And what a breakfast it was! Two fried eggs with bacon and sausages and an endless supply of hot buttered toast, all washed down with good strong tea. He reckoned it should keep his stomach quiet until he got back to London in time for supper at Sophie's home.

After he had eaten, he sat and read a newspaper until it was time to leave for Border Farm.

He had just heard the midday time signal on his car radio when he reached the crest of a ridge and saw the house nestling in a hollow two hundred yards ahead. It had a windbreak of trees on its farther side which gave the appearance of a theatre backdrop. The house itself was built of grey stone and partially covered by virginia creeper. It had a slate roof which looked like polished pewter in the sunlight.

At the bottom of the incline he was now descending, the track passed through an open gateway and broadened into an oval sweep of gravel in front of the house. He could see a large black dog lying across the stone step of the porch.

As he brought his car to a halt and got out, the dog rose slowly to its feet and came ambling across, its tail wagging a greeting. It was a labrador and well advanced in years from the greyness of its muzzle. He stooped to return its greeting with a friendly pat and it then walked ahead of him to the front door, which opened before he reached it.

'I saw your car coming,' a grey haired woman in a mauve dress said with a smile. 'I'm Barbara Hare and I assume you're Richard Deegan.' They shook hands and Richard followed her into the house. 'Barnaby makes a point of welcoming visitors,' she went on, giving the dog an affectionate glance. 'I think he lives in hope of one arriving with a sackful of marrow bones.'

'How old is he?'

'Fourteen. A real old man. You can't prise him away from the fire in the winter, but once the weather gets warm, the front step is his favourite place.' She pushed open a door and called out, 'Here's our visitor, Frank.'

Frank Hare was sitting in an upright chair, his crutches propped beside him. He turned his head and gave Richard a rueful smile.

'Forgive me if I don't get up, but I expect Ted told you I'm not very mobile these days.' He held out his hand. 'So you're Laurence Deegan's son! Can't see much resemblance.'

'I'm an adopted son.'

'Are you now! Well, that would explain the absence of resemblance.' He continued to gaze at Richard with an interested expression. 'Did your father and mother have no children of their own?'

'Yes, they had a son. My brother, Norris, who is two years older than me. He doesn't look like my father either. In fact, less than I do. And yet I sometimes see my father's expression when I'm staring in a mirror. I suppose it's a result of growing up under the same roof.'

Frank Hare nodded vaguely. 'Sit down there. My wife's gone to fetch the ice. She'll be back in a moment and then we can have a drink.'

Though he was now completely bald on top, he still had copper-coloured hair round the back and sides of his head. His complexion was fair and Richard could imagine the freckles his

144

grandmother had mentioned, though none were visible at the end of winter. He had lively blue eyes and a ready smile.

'So your father often used to talk about his army days, did he?' he said in a faintly ironic tone.

'Yes, quite a bit,' Richard said, wishing he wasn't the object of such an unwavering gaze. 'I believe you once spent a night at my grandmother's home in Colchester when you and Dad were coming on leave together.'

'I remember the occasion clearly. Is your grandmother still alive?'

'Yes, she lives at Bury St Edmunds. She's rather blind and has to have a companion, but otherwise she's fine for her age.'

'I recall her pumping me about our life in Germany as she complained that your father never used to tell her anything in his letters.' He glanced round as his wife came back bearing an ice bucket. 'What'll you have?'

'I'd love a beer.'

'A beer for our guest and I think I'll have the same just to be cussed.'

'I'd have done better to ask you before I fetched the ice,' Mrs Hare remarked without rancour. She handed them their drinks, poured herself a gin and tonic and said, 'I'll be in the kitchen if you want anything.'

Richard had the impression that her withdrawal was prompted more by tact than necessity.

'I was sorry to read of your father's death,' Frank Hare said. 'It must have come as a great shock to everyone.'

'Yes, it did. And the fact that he left no note made it that much worse. He was at the peak of his career and all set to become a judge and suddenly this happened.'

'Extraordinary,' Frank Hare murmured. Then fixing Richard with another unwavering look, he said, 'And what brings you to these parts?'

Richard was ready for the question and replied, 'I had to go up to Liverpool and thought I'd make my way back avoiding the motorways.'

'Shropshire still has the advantage of being moderately off the beaten track. This area, at least. What's your line of business? You're not a lawyer like your father, are you?'

'I'm a detective constable in the Metropolitan Police and attached to Special Branch.'

Frank Hare gave him a look of fresh interest. 'Enjoying it?'

'Very much.'

'Good for you. I'm sure the police can do with young men of your calibre. Did your parents encourage you to join?'

'It was my own idea, but they certainly didn't put any obstacles in my path. My brother, Norris, is a barrister.'

'I'm surprised to hear that your father used to reminisce about his national service days. I always had the impression that he didn't much care for them. But perhaps they became better in retrospect.'

'He used to talk about the wild times you had in the mess.'

'Oh, we certainly had those all right on Saturday nights. There were six of us little more than schoolboys, just commissioned and out of the egg. We must have been a pain in the neck to the older officers, but on the whole they were very tolerant of our bumptiousness.'

'Do you keep up with any of them?'

He shook his head. 'No, I haven't seen any of them since. Used to read about your father, of course, when he was appearing in some famous case or another. And there was one other fellow whose name pops up from time to time.'

'Tom Edward-Jones.'

He shot Richard a quizzical look. 'He was plain Tom Jones in those days. Did your father talk about him?'

'I don't think Dad cared for him. Mum certainly didn't. Nevertheless, Mr Edward-Jones was most anxious that Dad should defend his son who is due to be tried for murder. The brief was one of those that had to be returned after Dad's death.' Richard hesitated as he tried to decide whether to tell Frank Hare that he had met Tom Edward-Jones. Perhaps not for the moment. Instead he said, 'He sounded like a pretty lively figure in the mess.'

'That's one word for him.'

Richard waited, but when his host didn't enlarge on his somewhat enigmatic comment, he decided to prompt him.

'I gather you didn't care for him yourself?'

'No, I didn't. He was much too pushy for my liking. Always

trying to hold the floor and be our self-appointed leader. Mind you, he was resourceful and full of energy and in many ways a good subaltern. But he was also tactless and insensitive. He tried hard to cultivate the daredevil image. Often successfully. I accept that daredevils have their place in society, but they're a disturbing influence if you have to live with them. Anyway, he's done all right for himself since from all I've read.' He paused and, with a wry smile, added, 'You'll probably have gathered I couldn't stand him. It always seemed to me that your father fell a bit too much under his spell at times.'

'I'm fascinated by what you say, sir.'

'Justifies your visit, eh?' Frank Hare said with a challenging glance, so that Richard felt suddenly confused. 'Look, Richard,' his host went on, ' – by the way, you don't mind my calling you Richard? – my limbs may have seized up but my mind still functions pretty well and my guess is that you've made a special pilgrimage here to pump me about my knowledge of your father. From what you've told me since you came, I've put a further two and two together and my surmise is that you think your father's death may relate back to something which happened during that period. Am I right?'

'Absolutely right, sir,' Richard said in a relieved tone. 'I apologise for my clumsy subterfuge.'

Frank Hare appeared to wave aside the apology, muttering something that Richard didn't catch. 'I think, however,' he went on, 'that before I say anything further, you ought to tell me frankly what you have on your mind.'

It took Richard ten minutes to give his host a summary of events since his father's death.

'Do you have the photograph of the cigarette case with you?' Frank Hare enquired when Richard finished.

Richard fished inside his pocket. 'This is only a photograph of a photograph. The one I received is with the laboratory.'

'I would say that was your father's all right,' Hare said studying the photograph. 'He was the only one amongst us who had such an expensive case. Small wonder it was stolen.'

'Was Dad very upset?'

'I don't recall. You see, something happened about that time that took our minds off everything else.' For half a minute he stared out of the french window without speaking. Then slowly he returned his gaze to Richard. 'I don't know whether I'm doing the right thing or not in telling you this. It's highly defamatory and mayn't assist you as much as you think at first blush. Anyway, here goes.

'What happened was that a German girl from the nearby village suddenly disappeared and our unit came under suspicion, as it was known that she had been hanging around outside the main gate of our camp. The military police, as well as the local German police, conducted an investigation and we were all questioned about our movements the night she vanished. Personally, I found it a most disagreeable experience, but needless to say, Tom Jones regarded it as an additional excitement in our lives, which it may have been for him. The girl was never seen again and the assumption was that she'd been murdered and her body buried. There was no shortage of secret burial places in that area. It was heavily wooded and there were also a number of disused quarry workings. These were all searched and ponds were dragged, but there was no sign of the girl.'

'Mayn't she just have taken off? Wasn't it quite easy to lose oneself in Germany in the immediate post-war years?'

'True, but she was said to be a home-loving girl who wouldn't have acted in that way.'

'How old was she?'

'Seventeen.'

'And did suspicion fall on anyone in particular?' Richard asked, feeling a sudden dryness in his throat.

'On Tom Jones. Mind you, it *was* only suspicion, because not a scrap of evidence emerged to indicate that anyone in our unit had been involved. But Jones was the obvious suspect and he was certainly grilled harder than the rest of us by the military police. Again, that was largely his own fault, for, as I recall, he did his best to draw attention to himself, boasting of his prowess with girls and generally nudging everyone in the ribs. It was part of his act to regard the rest of us as timid mice who were too frightened to say boo to authority.'

'He must have been pretty unpopular.'

'I think I probably disliked him more than most. I know it used to irritate me that others didn't always appear to see him

148

for what he was. Certainly nobody loved him and yet he was never without a follower or two.'

'Was my father one of those?'

'Your father and he shared a hut, so he probably made more effort to get on with him for the sake of a tolerable life. But I didn't ever regard them as bosom friends. Jones didn't have friends of that sort.'

'But the fact that my father shared a hut with him . . .' Richard said bleakly.

'Don't misinterpret that! It wasn't from choice. We were paired off haphazardly. When someone new arrived, he occupied the vacant bed. If I remember aright that's what happened to your father and it happened to be in a hut with Jones.'

'Were you Dad's best friend at the time?'

'We got on well, but I don't think there were any particularly close friendships. There we were thrown together in a hutted camp outside a small country town in north Germany. We were worked hard and we did our best to enjoy ourselves in our spare time, though the facilities were fairly limited. Occasionally, there'd be an excuse to go swanning off to Hamburg or to Hanover, but for the most part our leisure was spent in the mess and at an officers' club in the town.'

'This girl you've mentioned, did she come from the town?'

'No, from a village in the opposite direction, which was about four miles from our camp.'

'Do you remember her name?'

'Gertrud Klose.'

'I wonder if her parents still live there?'

'I've no idea. But Klose is not an uncommon name. They were farming people, so perhaps they do still live there. On the other hand, thirty years is a long time to stay in one place.'

'You have,' Richard observed with a smile.

'True. We farmers tend to be less peripatetic than you city dwellers. You're not thinking of going out there, are you?'

'I'm not sure. If the girl has reappeared or her body has ever been found, I'd like to find out. I don't know whether the knowledge would help me, but it would, at least, tie up one loose end.'

'Well, I can save you a journey. There has never been any trace of her from that day to this. My wife and I were motoring

149

around that part of Germany two summers ago, visiting old haunts and my curiosity led me to make a discreet enquiry about Gertrud Klose. As I say, she's never been heard of again.'

'How did you find out?'

'I called at the office of the local newspaper. I didn't go looking for her family and thought it better not even to enquire after their whereabouts. I had no wish to excite other people's curiosity. I passed myself off as a writer researching a book on the theme of the occupying army's relations with the local population in the post-war years.'

Richard grinned. 'I'm glad to know that someone else stoops to subterfuge on occasion.'

'I got away with mine. Or, at least, I think I did.' Frank Hare turned his head toward the open door and sniffed. 'I smell lunch. You'll stay and have some with us, won't you?'

'I'd love to, though I feel I've already encroached too far on your kindness.'

'You'll have to eat somewhere before you drive back to London.'

'I'd been reckoning that Freda's breakfast would last me until evening,' Richard remarked with a smile.

'She knows how to fill a man's stomach all right. And so does my wife, particularly with Sunday lunch. We have a living-in couple, but this is their day off.'

It was three o'clock before Richard started on his homeward journey, after profuse thanks to the Hares for their hospitality. It was difficult to believe that only twenty-four hours had passed since he had set out from London.

As he threaded his way cross-country to join the motorway, he tried to draw up a balance sheet in respect of his expedition. On the credit side was the information he had gleaned about his father's time in the army. On the reverse side was the nature of that information, for whichever way he looked at it he could draw little comfort from what he had been told.

He realised he had been secretly hoping (even believing) that his father's name and reputation would, in the end, emerge unscathed, but it seemed an ever diminishing prospect.

It now appeared certain that his father's death was connected with an event in Germany thirty years previously and that Tom Edward-Jones had some part in it.

He reasoned that his father's sudden decision to return the Kulka brief could have been deliberately designed to mislead. To make everyone believe his death was related to something in the Official Secrets Act case, when in actual fact it had been the arrival of the brief to defend Terry Edward-Jones that had driven him to take his life. But why?

At that point, Richard stopped thinking and concentrated on all the Sunday afternoon drivers that the sun had brought forth. He fiddled with his car radio until he found a station pouring out schmaltzy music.

He felt himself in a state of suspended animation.

The Hares and Border Farm had dropped away behind him. like the runway behind a departing jet, and the realities awaiting him in London were far enough ahead to be ignored.

CHAPTER XX

Stanley always looked forward to the hour of half past ten each morning. By then everyone had departed for court and peace was restored after the preceding hectic fifty minutes when controlled panic had reigned. A panic composed of members picking up last minute briefs, trying to make urgent phone calls and generally all clamouring at once for their clerk's attention before taking off like bees from a hive. Moreover, it was always worse on a Monday morning, when somebody would find he had mislaid his robes or left his brief at home on the kitchen table or lost a volume of law reports vital to the case in hand. It all added up to panic and even though Stanley and his minions were accustomed to it, they were glad when it was over.

On this particular Monday, Chambers were deserted by half past ten apart from the clerks. Today there wasn't even anybody working on papers in his room. George Hallick had joined the exodus to go and make a plea in mitigation for a shoplifter at a magistrates' court but Stanley was in no mood to spare either the magistrate or George Hallick's client his sympathy.

John, the number two clerk, had gone over to the High Court on an errand and Mark, the junior clerk, was at the Old Bailey where three members of Chambers had cases that day.

Stanley lit a cigarette and let out a sigh of relief. As soon as John returned, he would go and meet a number of the Temple's senior clerks for coffee and a round-up of gossip.

He didn't hear the outer door open, but became suddenly aware of someone in the lobby outside. A moment later a shadow fell across the threshold of his room and a man appeared in the doorway. He was wearing a three quarter length coat and an astrakan hat which he now removed.

'Would you be Mr Beresford by any chance?'

'Yes.'

'Oh, good! My name's Powell. I'm from the Ministry of Defence.' He produced his identity card encased in its plastic holder and proffered it for Stanley's examination, while he glanced round the clerks' room with its permanent air of congestion. 'I wonder if I might have a quiet word with you somewhere?'

'Sit down, Mr Powell, we shan't be disturbed in here. Everybody's out except for me.'

Bernard Powell's expression was dubious, but after pointedly closing the door (which was usually kept permanently open) he sat down on a chair beside it, seemingly ready to repulse any intruders.

'It's about the late Laurence Deegan,' he said watching Stanley intently.

'I guessed so.'

'I suppose you would. You doubtless keep in touch with Mrs Deegan.'

'I do, though I've not spoken to her for ten days.'

'Oh! I thought she might have told you that I'd been to see her.' When Stanley remained silent, Powell assumed a grave expression, which he usually did when an interview failed to advance along the course he had charted for it. 'Did Mr Deegan leave many personal effects in Chambers?'

'Some,' Stanley said, after giving his visitor a surprised look.

'Would they still be here?'

'Yes.'

'So nobody's been through them yet?'

'I've emptied the drawers of his desk and put the contents in a packing case, which is still in his room. I've asked Mrs Deegan to let me know when she'd like to have it delivered to her.'

'What sort of effects are they?'

'Don't you think you ought to tell me why you're asking these questions, Mr Powell? Is it something to do with the Kulka case?'

'Yes, it is,' he said, leaning forward earnestly. 'There was a document in his brief which shouldn't have been there. A top

153

secret document that got in by mistake. All very embarrassing . . .'

'I returned the brief to the solicitors the day after Mr Deegan's death.'

'I know. The thing is that I phoned Mr Deegan privately the day before he died, explained what had happened and asked him to extract the document in question and keep it safely until I sent somebody to collect it. Regrettably the matter was overlooked in the aftermath of his sudden death. Hence my visit this morning.'

'Did you phone him here?' Stanley asked suspiciously.

'No, I took the liberty of calling him at home.'

'I'm sure there's no such document amongst any of his personal papers.'

'He would probably have left it in a sealed envelope and possibly have hidden it within the covers of a book.'

Stanley shook his head doubtfully.

'What I'd like to do with your permission,' Powell went on confidently, 'is make a quick search of things. As I know exactly what I'm looking for, it'll take less time that way.'

'I'm sorry, but I couldn't let you do that without Mrs Deegan's consent. She and Mr Deegan's solicitor are his executors and all his personal property is vested in them.'

Powell's brow creased in a small irritated frown. 'I think you're taking a more legalistic view than is called for. It won't take me more than a few minutes to look and, despite what you've just said, the document in question is not the property of his executors. It belongs to my ministry, so you see I'm only asking for the return of what is ours.'

'You can use my phone if you care to call Mrs Deegan and clear it with her,' Stanley said unmoved.

'You're putting me in a very awkward position, Mr Beresford. I'd hoped this was something we could deal with sensibly and without fuss.' He paused. 'Are you adamant that you won't let me take a quick look round Mr Deegan's room? If you're worried that somebody may find out, I assure you it won't be from me. Just give me five minutes and I'll be gone.'

'If it's as simple as that, why not call Mrs Deegan and explain?'

'This is not a matter I can properly discuss on the telephone,' he said stiffly. 'I'd have thought that was obvious from what I've said. However, I won't take up more of your time. I'm sorry I was unable to obtain your co-operation in an official matter.'

'Should I come across the document, do you wish me to get in touch with you?'

Powell bit his lip and hesitated before replying. 'I'll call you tomorrow. No point in giving you my telephone number as I shall be out most of the time.'

He had only briefly departed from Chambers when John returned.

'Who was that bloke I met on the stairs?' he asked.

'He was from the Ministry of Defence. Came to check on a document that found its way mistakenly into the Kulka brief.'

'A likely story!' John remarked with a laugh. 'I bet he was really after the petty cash.'

Stanley merely smiled, though he was as sceptical as John about the reason for Powell's visit, and with greater justification. Moreover, he had the advantage of having been forewarned about the man by Richard. He didn't believe for one moment that any document had been erroneously included in the brief. If there had been, he would almost certainly have noticed it when he glanced through the papers before locking them away in Laurence Deegan's safe. He was also certain that if Powell had phoned Deegan at home as he said he had done, head of Chambers would have mentioned this to him.

So if Powell had given a wholly false reason for wishing to make a search of Deegan's room, what was the truth? What was he really hoping to find?

A further sudden thought came into his mind. Supposing Powell had phoned Deegan at home the night before his death, could it have had anything to do with his rejection of the Kulka brief the next day and with his decision to kill himself?

The more he reflected on it, the more he saw Powell as a raven of ill omen.

CHAPTER XXI

Soon after Richard had reached his office that Monday morning, his telephone rang and Eddie's voice came on the line.

'I've news for you,' he said.

'Great! What is it?'

'I'd sooner not tell you over the phone. Meet me in the canteen in half an hour.'

'You sounded very mysterious,' Richard said, when he later sat down opposite his friend with a cup of coffee.

'Well, you know what a rumpus there can be if it's found out you've been making unofficial enquiries in C.R.O. The point is that the fingerprint on the photograph you gave me has been identified. It came up better than I'd expected and there was enough for a check to be made. It was part of the right thumb print of one Tom Edward-Jones.' He shot Richard a quick look. 'You don't seem surprised.'

'I am and I'm not. I guessed it was he who sent the photograph, but I'm more than interested to learn he's on file in C.R.O. What for?'

'Indecent assault back in 1958. He was charged with attempted rape, but pleaded guilty to the lesser offence and was fined a hundred pounds. It can't have been a terribly bad case.'

'Either that or he struck lucky with the judge. Anyway, thanks a lot, Eddie, you've been a great help.'

Eddie drained his cup and slid it with well-judged accuracy to the end of the table where a female was collecting them on a tray. 'I must shoot off,' he said, jumping to his feet. 'We're busier than a society photographer in Ascot week. See you.'

Richard finished his own coffee and returned to his office.

In the light of what he had learnt yesterday from Frank Hare, it was highly significant that Tom Edward-Jones had a criminal conviction for a sexual offence. It was a further indication of his involvement with Gertrud Klose, for there could be little doubt that a sexual motive lay behind her disappearance and presumed murder.

He was still assessing this latest piece of information when his telephone rang again. This time his caller was Detective Sergeant Angelo of Wimbledon.

'Are you still interested in Terry Edward-Jones?' he asked, after a brief exchange of pleasantries.

'Very much so, though I'm having to keep my interest under wraps these days.'

'That's O.K., I shan't tell anyone, but listen to this and tell me what you make of it? I had to go to Brixton prison on Saturday to serve some papers on a prisoner. He knew I was involved in the Edward-Jones case and told me he had recently spent a number of days in the next bed to him in the prison hospital. He said that Master Terry was very depressed and had lost all his bounce. It seems he's no longer confident of a triumphant acquittal and is sunk in black despair at the prospect of a spell inside. Now comes the part that'll interest you. His change of attitude stems from the fact that your father will no longer be defending him.'

'It makes it sound as if my father was the only counsel who got people off,' Richard observed, as he tried to make sense of what he had just been told.

'There are too many of them around, if you ask me. But it seems that Terry was doing no more than reflect his old man's views. Apparently Tom E-J visits him regularly and it was he who sowed this seed of despondency in sonny's ear. According to Blythe – that's the chap I was visiting – Terry had said he'd been bound to get off if your father had defended him because he'd have had a much stronger defence. Sounds cockeyed to me, but I'm merely passing it on as Blythe told it. Needless to say, as far as I'm concerned, it's all good news. But then I'm not a member of the Terry Edward-Jones fan club. I hope he'll be

157

convicted and go to prison and his father won't be able to buy him out of trouble. Anyway, I thought you'd be interested.'

'I am. Thanks for phoning me. As you say, it sounds pretty cockeyed. If you hear anything more, let me know.'

'I may do as I shall have to go and see Blythe again. It's just been discovered that the forms I've served on him have a couple of wrong dates in their particulars and fresh ones have had to be re-typed. He's a nasty piece of work is Blythe, but he's a great tongue-wagger when he's in trouble. A natural grass who'll end up on a mortuary slab before he's much older.'

For some time after Detective Sergeant Angelo had rung off, Richard was lost in thought. Disagreeable thought. He wondered whether it had been as obvious to Angelo as it had been to him that Terry Edward-Jones could only have meant that his father would have been a party to a concocted defence. And if that inference were correct, it was a further indication of the pressure Tom Edward-Jones was proposing to put on his son's counsel. A counsel he had personally chosen for the invidious task of defending his son.

But what could have been the nature of that pressure?

Not for the first time, Richard found himself shying away from the logical conclusion of his thoughts. On this occasion he was assisted by the sudden arrival of Detective Constable Tinkler who burst into the room with a sheaf of papers in one hand and an umbrella in the other.

'*En garde,*' he cried, hurling the papers on to his desk and making a lunge at Richard with the umbrella.

'What's the excitement?' Richard enquired in a faintly weary tone.

'Can't you see, I've found my umbrella!'

'I didn't know you'd lost it.'

Pat Tinkler paused in his antic and gave Richard a pitying look. 'It's not really mine, stupid. When did you ever see me carrying an umbrella?'

'I didn't think I had.'

'It's Monday morning, but you're still in Sunday. I wouldn't mind owning one like this, however. It can do practically everything except discharge a ground to air nuclear missile. It can fire a .22 bullet out of one end. It has a radio transmitter and

158

receiver in the handle and a small camera in this slot here. It can also be used for keeping off the rain.'

'Where on earth did it come from?' Richard asked in an intrigued voice.

'You'll never guess. It was handed in to the lost property office at Waterloo Station. It was found by a porter yesterday on a train that had arrived from Southampton. The man in the office was checking it, when, bang, a bullet came out of the pointed end. Luckily, it missed his foot and embedded itself in the floor. The railway police were informed and I was sent to fetch it this morning.' He gave it another flourish. 'Don't worry, it's unloaded now and has also been checked for fingerprints.'

'Were any found?'

Tinkler shook his head. 'The owner may have been a bit forgetful, but at least he remembered to wear gloves.'

'Wonder whose it is?'

'It's definitely of foreign origin, as they say, but I scarcely think the owner's likely to come forward and claim it. The anti-terrorist squad want to have a look at it and then it's going to the lab for examination.'

'I wonder what the chap thought when he discovered he'd mislaid it.'

'I know,' Tinkler said with a grin. 'And on a Sunday too. Not even as if he could go out and buy another.' He turned to leave. 'If my phone rings, say I'll be back in about an hour. What are you doing for lunch, Richard?'

'Nothing.'

'Let's go and have a pint together. But if I'm not back by one o'clock, don't hang about.'

In fact, it was Richard who later left a note on Pat Tinkler's desk saying that he had had to go and meet his brother.

Norris telephoned just after twelve. He sounded tense and worried and said he wanted to talk to Richard urgently and would meet him anywhere if he, Richard, couldn't make it to the Temple. As it was rare for his brother to make such spontaneous offers, Richard accepted and suggested a pub not far from St James' Park underground station.

Norris was already in the pub when Richard arrived. He was tucked away in a corner and wearing an affronted expression.

'God knows how we can possibly talk in this crowd,' he remarked, as Richard reached him.

'All pubs are the same at lunchtime,' Richard said peaceably. 'Why don't we have a drink and a sandwich and then we can go and walk round the park? It's almost warm enough to sit out.'

'It'll be better to walk. I don't fancy squeezing on to a bench with fidgeting children.'

'As you wish. Meanwhile, as this is my territory, what'll you have?'

To Richard's disgust, Norris said he'd have a small dry sherry and one sausage on a stick. Richard had nothing against dry sherry, but he didn't reckon it to be a young man's lunchtime drink in a pub. As it was Norris had finished his meal almost before his brother had begun and then stood in stony silence while Richard munched his way through two cold beef sandwiches which he washed down with a pint of draught beer.

'Ready?' Norris asked, while Richard was still swallowing his last mouthful. 'I normally have lunch in my Inn,' he said, alluding to his Inn of Court. 'It's rather more civilised than a pub.'

If you can put up with a lot of boring young barristers, Richard felt like saying but refrained. There was no point as Norris was one of them himself when in their company.

They walked in silence until they reached the park and began their perambulation round the lake. The air was mild and all the ducks and wild fowl knew as well as everyone else that spring had come at last. Even the pelicans were sunning themselves on the bank like wise old men in solemn conclave.

'I'm sorry, Richard, but I've just got to talk to you,' Norris said in a tight voice, once he was satisfied there was nobody within earshot. 'Mother obviously won't, so I must, even if it means having a bit of a showdown. It's about your investigation into Father's death.'

'So I assumed,' Richard murmured.

'I'd hoped it wouldn't come to this, but you've left me with no alternative by going on with your ill-conceived enquiries.' He paused and Richard observed him compress his lips in a rigid line of disapproval. 'What I'm about to tell you, I haven't breathed to another soul. Not even Joanna knows. I know how fond you were of Father's and I'm afraid it's going to come as a nasty shock to you, but that's partly your own fault. And I'll be quite frank with you, Richard, my main concern is number one. Yes, myself. It's my career I'm thinking of, because if what I tell you should ever become public knowledge, I might as well pack up at the Bar and emigrate.'

Richard shot his brother a puzzled glance. Norris had always been given to over-dramatizing events which affected him. It was a reflection of his lack of a sense of humour. Even as a small boy he had tended to take himself far too seriously.

'So before I do say anything,' he now went on, 'I want your word of honour that you'll never tell another living person. Not Mother, nor Sophie and especially nobody in your department.' He turned his head and fixed Richard with an intense look. 'Do you now give me your word?'

Richard didn't reply immediately and was suddenly aware that he was walking on his own. He stopped and looked back to see Norris standing stock still, staring after him. When he didn't move, Richard retraced his steps.

'I'm not moving,' Norris said in a portentous tone, 'until I have your word. I'm not joking, Richard, I mean it.'

'How can I give you my word of honour when I have no idea what you're going to tell me?'

'I'm going to tell you why Father committed suicide, which means you'll have no further need to continue your own investigation. Does that satisfy you?'

Richard gave his brother a startled look. If it had come from anyone other than Norris, he would have assumed it was some sort of try-on. But he could see that his brother was in deadly earnest. Tension was reflected in every feature.

'All I've ever wanted to find out is why Dad did it. If you give me a convincing reason, I agree that my quest will be at an end. I don't know, however, why you couldn't have told me sooner; assuming you've known for some time.'

'That'll become clear in due course. I take it I have your word?'

'You have my word that I won't divulge anything which could be hurtful to Dad's name and reputation.'

'Good enough!' Glancing quickly about him, he went on in

a hushed whisper, 'Have you ever heard of the Brotherhood of Racial Purity?'

Richard nodded. 'It's an extremist right-wing organisation.'

'Father was a member,' Norris said bleakly.

Richard stared at him in disbelief. 'He can't have been. He was a liberal in every sense of the word. He was closer to the left than the right.'

'You'd hardly have expected him to boast of membership of a group as dangerous and disreputable as the Brotherhood of Racial Purity. It wouldn't have done his practice any good and it would have killed outright his prospects of becoming a judge. His support of moderate political opinion was part of the act to throw anyone off the scent. You probably know more about the Brotherhood than I do, Richard, but I read somewhere that it was their policy in infiltrate the upper echelons of society and have their sympathisers in important places in the professional and business world.' He paused. 'I don't know whether you recall, but Father defended one of their members about two years ago and got him off. He'd been charged with inciting racial hatred.'

Richard nodded thoughtfully. 'Yes, I do remember. But Dad also appeared for Communists and Marxists in his time. Surely you're not suggesting that he only represented those with whom he was politically in tune?'

'Of course I'm not,' Norris replied sharply. 'I mentioned it as being one small bit of evidence.'

'I wouldn't call it evidence at all.'

Norris frowned. 'Perhaps you'll reserve your judgement until I've told you the rest.'

'Go ahead! So far you've merely made a bald statement without anything to back it up.' Richard's tone verged on the scornful and two spots of colour appeared on Norris' cheeks.

'You don't think I'd make such an allegation without evidence?' he remarked tartly.

'I'm listening.'

'One evening about six months ago I called on Father in Chambers, as I wished to discuss a personal matter with him.' Richard thought he knew what the personal matter was, for he recalled his mother telling him that Norris had sought to borrow money from his father. 'While I was there,' Norris went on,

162

'Father went along to the clerks' room and I happened to notice a scrap of paper on his desk on which he had scribbled, "8.30 p.m. tonight B.R.P." I was trying to work out what B.R.P. stood for when I noticed the corner of a cyclostyled sheet sticking out from beneath his leather blotter. I lifted the blotter and saw the words Brotherhood of Racial Purity with an address in Chiswick. I didn't have time to read any more before he came back into the room. I couldn't believe he was a member; on the other hand, there was the notice and the scrap of paper which seemed to indicate a meeting that very evening. As soon as he sat down at his desk, he obviously noticed the scrap of paper for he quickly folded it in two and stuck it in his pocket, giving me a very odd look as he did so, as if to see whether I reacted in any way. Needless to say, I didn't.' Norris moistened his lips. 'If I hadn't happened to read this article in a magazine about a month before, I probably wouldn't have taken any notice. But it described what a dangerous and unscrupulous organisation it was and how it kept its members in line by threatening to expose them if they tried to backslide.' He shot Richard a meaningful glance. 'I'm sure the significance of that doesn't escape you. It's obvious to me that it was the threat of exposure that drove Father to take his life. He realised he was chained to a time-bomb. He wanted to get out, but couldn't without having his career blown apart. And the longer he remained a member, the more enmeshed he became.'

'These two pieces of paper you saw on his desk aren't positive proof he was a member of the Brotherhood,' Richard said cautiously.

'Wait until you hear the rest!' Norris retorted. 'That evening I went to the address in Chiswick, or rather I stood in the shadows on the opposite side of the street. The house in question was a Victorian semi-detached with nothing to distinguish it from its neighbours. I watched about half a dozen people arrive. All male and of varying ages, so far as I could tell in the dark. Father arrived alone on foot. Like the others, he just pressed the bell and the door was opened immediately as if there was someone on duty just inside.'

'How long did the meeting last?'

'I didn't stay. I'd found out all I needed to know. I'd satisfied myself that Father really was a member.' He gave Richard a faintly triumphant look. 'When I arrived home, I phoned the parents' flat. Mother answered and when I enquired if Father was there, she said he'd had to go out to pay his respects to some eminent Swiss lawyer who'd flown in for a high-powered consultation next day. She mentioned that she expected him back soon after eleven. Do you believe me now, Richard?'

'It's wholly incredible. There must be some explanation.'

'There is! The one staring you in the face. He *was* a member, and in deep trouble. It's the only possible explanation. Moreover, why do you think this man, Powell, visited Mother? Obviously because they'd got on to Father's activities and didn't want amateurs like you, Richard, trampling over their scenery. You have to admit that it all makes sense. Believe me, I've had six months to live with it and there's no escaping the conclusion.' They had almost completed their circuit of the lake when once more Norris halted abruptly in his tracks and waited for Richard to turn back. 'Now do you see why nobody must ever know?' he said urgently. 'It would kill Mother, wreck my career and leave us social outcasts.'

'Oh, really!' Richard expostulated.

'Well, it would certainly be a long time before I felt able to lift my head again.'

'I agree it's not something one would like to have noised abroad.'

Norris let out a deep-felt sigh. 'I'm very relieved to hear you say that. Quite frankly, I've dreaded telling you for fear you . . .'

'For fear I what?'

'I don't know what I thought you might do. You're such a tenacious fellow, I've been terrified where your enquiries might lead you and what you might unearth. In the end, I decided it was worth taking the risk and telling you what I knew, rather than have you innocently involve us all in a public scandal.'

'Thank you for your confidence,' Richard said in a tone of heavy irony.

'I'm not going to apologise, Richard. As I said, I've not even told Joanna and I wouldn't have told you if I could have thought of some other way of warning you off. But now you know and I hope it's a secret which'll go with us to the grave.' He kicked at a pebble which rolled into the water. 'I'm not being wise after the event, but I often felt there was something a bit immature about Father.'

Richard stared at his brother's back with conflicting emotions. If what Norris had told him was true (and he had no reason to disbelieve the actual facts) it explained a number of things that had hitherto mystified him. But it didn't explain everything; for instance, why his father had chosen that particular moment to bring his life to such a dramatic end. Richard still felt there must be a connection between his death and something which had happened that very day.

It was conceivable, of course, that he had received a telephone call after Stanley had left Chambers and he was alone in the building. But that didn't entirely accord with the earlier display of strange behaviour.

Could it be that he himself had made a call that had precipitated events? If he already had the call in mind when he walked back to Chambers from the Old Bailey in Stanley's company, it could account for his air of preoccupation.

Norris was now several yards ahead of him and Richard quickened his step. Of one thing he was sure, his father could never voluntarily have become involved in anything as pernicious and evil as the Brotherhood of Racial Purity. Norris might choose to believe it, but he never would.

Nevertheless, it was with his mind in greater turmoil than ever that he walked back to the Yard.

CHAPTER XXII

After an afternoon spent trying unsuccessfully to concentrate on a report he had to write, Richard was about to leave and go and pick up Sophie when his phone rang and he received peremptory instructions to accompany a detective chief inspector to Victoria Station and keep watch on the movements of a suspected Red Brigade terrorist who was believed to be on the boat train from Dover. The port police had been uncertain of their identification and had notified Special Branch at the Yard.

Detective Chief Inspector Glassford, who knew the man, was glumly silent as he and Richard set out for the railway station. This suited Richard who felt in no mood to talk. He had been obliged to call Sophie and cancel their arrangement and he had the strong feeling that he had been deliberately singled out for the assignment as part of a policy to keep Detective Constable Deegan's nose hard against the grindstone.

The D.C.I. had proposed that they should walk to the station and Richard had agreed. Not that there was really any choice. If the D.C.I. wanted to walk, that was that, unless he could plead a developing hernia or a blistered heel.

They reached the station concourse and scrutinised the arrival board. The train wasn't due for another fifteen minutes and they ascertained that it was expected to be no more than five minutes late.

'We'll go and have a word with the railway police,' Chief Inspector Glassford said with a melancholy sigh. 'Better let them know we're here in case we need their assistance.'

The D.C.I., who could speak fluent French and Italian, had

166

an encyclopaedic knowledge of Europe's splintered terrorist organisations. He was also regarded as one of Special Branch's mild eccentrics.

When they returned to the concourse after informing the railway police of their mission, D.C.I. Glassford said suddenly, 'I knew your father slightly. He was very kind to me on one occasion, well before you joined S.B.'

'Where did you meet him?' Richard asked with interest and when it became apparent the D.C.I.'s attention had strayed elsewhere.

'Sorry, I was observing that big chap over there with the blond beard. I thought for a moment it was a Swede, named Sigurd Wennström, who used to be mixed up with an offshoot of the Baader-Meinhof crowd. But I can see now it's not him. Where did I meet your father?' he echoed, focussing his gaze on Richard as if becoming suddenly aware of his presence. 'It was one of those matters that never reached Court. A left-wing M.P., who shall remain nameless, but who's no longer in parliament, was involved. I overstepped the mark somewhat in my enquiries and found myself out on a limb. If it had not been for your father, I could have finished up in a lot of trouble. I've always been grateful to him.'

'How did he help you?'

'The M.P. consulted your father and there was an internal enquiry, but honour was able to be satisfied without any heads rolling. I say heads in the plural, but, in fact, my own was the only one at risk. It was thanks to your father's tactful handling of his angry client, who wanted my head served up on a charger like John the Baptist's, that I survived.'

'Was that the only time you met him?'

D.C.I. Glassford gave Richard a dreamily thoughtful look. 'From what I hear, you took your father's death pretty hard, though I don't know why anyone should have expected otherwise. I imagine he was a good father and to have him die by his own hand without explanation must have come as a cruel shock.'

'It did,' Richard said quietly.

'Was that the only time I met him, I think you asked?' D.C.I. Glassford went on, as if plucking the question from a bran tub. But before he could answer, he started forward. 'Here comes our train. Remember if it's him, he's shaved off his beard, so look for a small scar at the right corner of his mouth.'

Ten minutes later he said sadly, 'Well, if he was on the train, we've missed him. Either it wasn't him at all or he jumped off somewhere along the line. There was certainly nobody resembling the man I know, bearded or unbearded.' He gave Richard a wan smile. 'You go off home. I'll get back to the Yard. Sorry it was a wasted effort.'

Before Richard could say anything, D.C.I. Glassford was striding purposefully toward the station exit. Richard stared after him with a faintly bemused expression. He might be an eccentric, but he was a kind-hearted one.

CHAPTER XXIII

Richard pulled up outside Sophie's home at ten minutes to eight the next morning. She opened the front door almost immediately. Katie was just behind her and pulled a face when Richard and Sophie kissed.

'What's wrong with you?' Richard enquired.

'I think it's yukky kissing at breakfast time.'

'Oh, is that all!'

'No, will you give me a lift to school, Richard?'

'You'll be there much too early if you come with us.'

'That's what I keep telling her,' Sophie chimed in.

'I don't mind,' Katie said belligerently.

Richard shrugged. 'You can come as far as I'm concerned, provided you're ready.'

Katie's school was about a mile away and she normally went by bus. Today squashed triumphantly into the back seat of Richard's car, she beamed her superiority at people waiting at every bus stop.

After she had been decanted outside her school, Richard felt freer to tell Sophie of his previous day's activity. He mentioned having met Norris for lunch, but refrained from recounting what his brother had told him. He would like to have done so, but he had given Norris his word and would keep it.

Sophie had had no further scary experiences and it seemed likely that Tom Edward-Jones must be satisfied that his brief campaign of intimidation had paid off. Richard's letter would, of course, have confirmed that.

But the great unanswered question remained. Why had he wanted to prevent Richard making his enquiries?

After dropping Sophie outside her place of work, he parked his car and walked the final lap of his journey to Scotland Yard.

Pat Tinkler was already in when Richard arrived.

'Detective Sergeant Angelo of Wimbledon phoned five minutes ago and I said you'd call him back,' he said, without looking up from the soft porn magazine that held his interest. 'She's not bad, not bad at all,' he murmured, as he gazed at a double spread of a nude blonde. 'Some of them should have been pensioned off years ago. There's one who looks old enough to be a grandmother.'

'Waste of money, those magazines.'

'You don't think I bought this, do you?' Tinkler said indignantly. 'I'll have you know that I'm studying it in the course of duty.'

'Oh, yes!'

'I mean it, Richard. There's been a suggestion that the small ads at the back are being used by the I.R.A. to pass messages to cells in this country.'

'And are they?'

'Not unless vibrator denotes a machine pistol and booster jelly is really gelignite, which it isn't if the picture of the girl applying it to her fanny is anything to go by.' He closed the magazine and pushed it from him. 'How'd you get on with old Glassford last night?'

'The chap wasn't on the train after all.'

'He's a rum one, isn't he? Old Glassford, I mean. Talking to him is a bit like driving a car with a slipping clutch. But he's a nice man, which is more than you can say for some we both know'.

Richard nodded. 'I'd better call Angelo or he'll be out.'

'People on division are never in,' Pat Tinkler said, heading for the door. 'Not when you want them, that is.'

Detective Sergeant Angelo, however, was at his desk and answered immediately.

'I was at Brixton prison again yesterday afternoon,' he said, 'and I picked up a bit more gossip from Blythe. I gather Terry

170

E-J is still very depressed. He told Blythe how unlucky he'd been and how he'd have got away with it if the girl's body hadn't been discovered so quickly. It seems his dad was all ready to dispose of it, but it was found before he could do anything.'

'What exactly was he going to do?'

'Remove it and dump it somewhere, I imagine. He'd hardly have been likely to try and bury it on Wimbledon Common where she was killed.'

'I wonder,' Richard murmured to himself.

'Wonder what?'

'I was talking to myself.'

'Some dad who's prepared to dispose of his son's dead bodies!' Sergeant Angelo observed. 'Talk about clearing up after the kids!'

'Might Blythe be called as a prosecution witness?'

'Not a hope! You know how jumpy the lawyers get at the suggestion of calling someone to give evidence of confidences exchanged in prison cells. Anyway, this latest isn't so much evidence as an indication of the sort of family he comes from. I might try and push our counsel if Blythe ever came up with an actual confession of murder Terry had made to him. But I'm not sure even then. The trouble with Blythe is that the devil himself wouldn't care to accept his word that he had two horns and a forked tail, without checking in a mirror. It'd be a waste of time to put him in the witness box. Well, I must go across to court, I'm giving evidence myself this morning.'

'Thanks again,' Richard said.

'Don't mention it. You'd better come along to the trial if you're all that interested.'

But that was something Richard had no intention of doing.

After picking up Sophie that evening, they drove to his mother's flat.

'I'm taking your advice and going away,' Fay said soon after they'd arrived. 'I spoke to Ruth on the phone this morning and we're going to Torquay for a week. Her doctor has recommended she should have some sea air to assist her convalescence and I said I'd go with her.'

171

'I'm delighted to hear it, Mum,' Richard said. 'Pity you're not going somewhere warmer.'

'I'm sure Torquay will be as warm as anywhere in this country. Anyway, neither of us feels up to a long journey, so it'll suit us very well. I'll have the car and we shall be able to explore the countryside. It's years since I was in Devon and I'm looking forward to it.'

'Why not go for two weeks? I'm sure Aunt Ruth would stay longer.'

'I suspect that a week is as long as we can comfortably tolerate each other's company.'

'You mean, that you can put up with her.'

'Perhaps I do. In any event, I oughtn't to be away longer as I gather the solicitors are making progress with your father's estate and will be wanting me to sign things.'

If Richard knew his father's solicitors, it would still be a long drawn-out affair with lengthy silences punctuated by letters which took the matter an inch forward at a time. But he realised that his mother had conjured up the demands of lawyers as an excuse for not staying away longer and so he made no comment.

They had been talking just inside the living-room, but now his mother and Sophie went and sat down, leaving Richard to attend to drinks.

Speaking over his shoulder, he said, 'I meant to ask you before, Mum, have you ever heard of the Brotherhood of Racial Purity.'

'Didn't your father once have a case involving one of their members? I seem to recall his saying they were one of the country's more obnoxious groups. He hated extremists of all sorts.'

'That was certainly always my impression.'

'He was a born middle-of-the-road man.'

'When Sophie and I went to see Grannie, she was saying what a secretive boy he was and how nothing could be prised out of him unless he wanted. I'd never thought of him that way.'

'It was probably his protective shell against her. She's always been a strong-minded woman and she'd have managed his life if she'd been given half a chance.' With a touch of acerbity, she

172

added, 'Her mother-in-law face and her grannie face haven't always been the same, Richard.'

'I've realised that. But getting back to Dad, did you ever consider him secretive?'

His mother was thoughtful for a while. Then in a reflective tone, she said, 'Some people are patently secretive. Others don't give that impression, but it doesn't mean that they tell you everything. I'd put your father in the second category.' After a further pause, she went on, 'There was a time when I'd have said there were no secrets between us. Now, I'm not so sure.'

'Is that a view you've reached since his death?' Richard asked gently.

'It's been crystallised by his death,' she said, staring bleakly into the fireplace.

For the first time, Richard realised the appalling trauma his father's death must have caused her. He had known, of course, that she'd been shocked and distressed, but she had borne up so well, he had overlooked the terrible crisis of faith it must have brought her. It must have rocked the very foundations of her life with the ferocity of a cyclone. The man with whom she had lived for twenty-seven years had not only abruptly deserted her, but had chosen to do so in the most devastating manner. It was remarkable in the circumstances that she had managed to retain any composure at all. This thought was still uppermost in Richard's mind when she spoke again.

'What more have you found out, Richard?'

He pulled a dejected face and shook his head.

'But you're not giving up?' she added.

'Of course not.'

'That's all right, then.'

He gave her a sharp look. 'You really are glad I'm going on?'

'I'd like you to get to the bottom of the mystery,' she said.

'There's no guarantee that I ever shall, Mum. At times I seem to be going round in tight circles.' He fell silent for a moment. 'You said originally you didn't want to know anything that might show Dad in an unfavourable light; is that how you still feel?'

'Yes. I rely on you not to tell me anything you consider I wouldn't want to know.'

Richard had long thought that should he ever reach the end of his quest, this could prove the most worrisome problem of all.

'Incidentally, Mum, better not tell Norris that I'm still probing away. He wouldn't approve.'

'I know. He's made it very clear to me that he disapproves most strongly of what you're doing.'

Later when they were leaving, Richard tried to persuade his mother to join him and Sophie for a cheap meal at a small Greek restaurant they sometimes frequented. But she declined on the ground that there was a television programme she wanted to watch.

It was around midnight when Richard arrived home and went straight to bed. Normally, however troublesome the day had been, he would fall asleep immediately, but not so this night. He turned restlessly from one side to the other, his mind swirling like a fast-flowing river.

If he valued his career in the police, there was probably nothing further he could do to probe either his father's connection with the Brotherhood of Racial Purity or the mystery of his presence at parties given by the Czech Embassy. Moreover, it was hard to see how the two matters could be reconciled.

On the other hand, if Norris was wrong in his analysis of what had happened (and Richard somehow believed he was without having any contrary evidence), then he was brought back to the Edward-Jones connection.

Ever since his visit to Shropshire, he had realised that he would not be able to get any further without a confrontation with Tom Edward-Jones. It was either that or an admission of defeat.

At least he now had some ammunition to fire at Edward-Jones, but it would still be a course of action fraught with all manner of risks. Anyone as powerful and ruthless as Tom Edward-Jones wouldn't hesitate to lash out if he felt himself endangered. For a start, he was likely to be angry at discovering that Richard hadn't ceased his investigation.

But the main problem Richard faced was having no idea why Edward-Jones had tried to deter him in the first place. There had to be a reason, which he was apparently determined to keep hidden and which, at the same time, bore on his father's suicide.

If he did confront Tom Edward-Jones, it was going to be like a game of chess, with hand-grenades for pieces.

After considering various ways of effecting a meeting, he decided that the simplest was probably the best. He would telephone him in the morning and make an appointment.

With this settled in his mind, he fell asleep.

CHAPTER XXIV

Nobody had ever accused Richard of having an over vivid imagination, but even he had not expected his attempt to meet Tom Edward-Jones to be achieved in quite such mundane fashion. In the event, it turned out to be no more difficult than making an appointment to see the dentist. He couldn't help feeling a sense of anti-climax.

The same cool-voiced secretary had answered the telephone and had asked him to hang on when he said he wished to see Mr Edward-Jones. Admittedly he had then had to wait for at least two minutes before her voice came on the line again.

'If you like to come here about half past six this evening, Mr Edward-Jones could see you,' she had said. 'He'll be up in his flat.'

'Where's that?'

'You know E-J House in Park Lane? His flat is on the sixth floor. There's a private lift that'll take you straight up. Come to the main entrance and the security guard will show you.'

After he had rung off, Richard was left wondering why he had bothered to lie awake trying to evolve a strategy when a simple knock on the door was all that had been required.

It was inconceivable that he could come to any physical harm. Tom Edward-Jones might be a common thug beneath his West End veneer, but he would hardly indulge in skulduggery in his Park Lane flat. Moreover, he presumably employed others to do any dirty work, such as young men to frighten the wits out of girls on pedestrian crossings and make crude telephone threats. The danger time, if such was to be, would come later, after their meeting had taken place. Nevertheless, he would tell Sophie where he was going, just in case anything should happen.

E-J House was a modern building at the top end of Park Lane. It wasn't large compared with others in the neighbourhood, but it lacked nothing in opulence.

The foyer was thickly carpeted in burgundy red and was dominated by a huge glass-topped desk on which rested three telephones of different colours. Tall vases of flowers stood on pedestals, which were artfully lit from beneath, and two long black sofas, which must have cost a king's ransom, were placed at right angles to each other with a low marble table as their companion.

All this Richard took in as he pushed through the heavy glass outer door. Behind the desk sat a burly young man in a blue uniform with security flashes on his shoulders.

He watched impassively as Richard approached.

'Mr Edward-Jones is expecting me,' Richard said, aware that his mouth had gone suddenly dry.

'Are you Mr Deegan?'

'Yes.'

The young man reached for the red telephone and lifted the receiver.

'Mr Deegan's here, sir,' he announced after a second's wait. 'Very good, sir.' He looked up at Richard. 'It's the lift on the far right,' he said pointing with a powerful finger. Indeed, his hands looked as capable of crushing rocks as most people's are of splintering match boxes.

As Richard neared the lift, its doors opened and he realised it had been operated from the desk. Inside, he pushed the button labelled 'penthouse' and the door closed with a soft sigh. At the top he stepped out into a small and apparently hermetically sealed lobby with one solid-looking door straight ahead. A moment later, Tom Edward-Jones stood staring at him with a quizzical expression.

'Come in,' he said.

He led the way into a large living-room, one side of which was entirely window with a terrace beyond.

'A drink? A vodka and tonic I seem to remember.'

'Thank you.'

'I got your letter.'

'Yes.'

'You said you'd given up your enquiries, so what is it you want to talk about?'

'Since I sent you that letter, various things have happened,' Richard said, bracing himself for what he felt was about to be a plunge into shark-infested water.

'Go on.'

'I've met Frank Hare.'

'Hare? Hare? Is that someone I ought to know?'

'He was in the army in Germany with you and my father.'

'A freckled, red-haired chap?'

'Yes.'

'And what did he have to tell you?' Tom Edward-Jones asked warily.

'That you and my father shared a hut.'

'True. So what?'

'He also told me about a German girl who disappeared and was never seen again. Gertrud Klose.'

'Well, go on.' His tone was faintly hectoring.

'I want to know what happened to her.'

'Why do you suppose I know?'

'Frank Hare said you came under suspicion and that you hinted you could tell the police more if you were minded to.'

Edward-Jones let out a disagreeable laugh, 'Oh, I could certainly have done that, though I doubt whether your father would have thanked me if I had. Look, Richard, I warned you not to dabble, but, despite what you wrote in your letter, you've obviously gone on doing so. Don't blame me if you don't like what you find out. Meanwhile, my advice to you is still the same. Go away and forget what's happened.'

'I have to know the truth. I believe you were responsible for my father committing suicide.'

'Oh yes? And how do you work that out?'

'I believe you killed Gertrud Klose. Moreover, I believe you stole my father's cigarette case and used it to incriminate him in her death.'

178

'You're making very dangerous accusations which could land you in a lot of trouble,' Edward-Jones said in a tone of cold scorn. 'If Hare has put you up to this, he'll also find himself in trouble. I hope you'll both be able to find the sort of damages I'll be awarded for such fanciful and slanderous statements.'

Richard swallowed hard. He hadn't expected it to be a comfortable meeting, but at least he was still afloat. In an even tone, he went on:

'You left a thumb-print on the photograph of my father's cigarette case which you so thoughtfully sent me.' As he spoke he had the satisfaction of Edward-Jones' reaction. It was as if he had received a sharp blow on the point of his chin. For a while he stared hard at Richard, apparently trying to decide whether he was being bluffed. But he must have realised that his reaction had already betrayed him for he gave an impatient shrug.

'It was for your own good,' he said harshly.

'Was it also for my own good that you got someone to try and intimidate my girl-friend?'

'I don't know what you're talking about,' he said, without either surprise or any attempt at conviction.

'When you invited me to the Croesus Club, your real interest was in discovering how much I knew about my father's time in the army,' Richard went on determinedly. 'You wanted to find out whether he'd talked about what happened in Germany. When I said he hadn't, it must have come as a relief to you, but you were still anxious lest I should go on investigating and find out about Gertrud Klose's death. That's why you first gave me friendly advice and then backed it up with threats.'

'You're talking rubbish.'

'I think not. After all, disposing of bodies is something that comes quite naturally to you, isn't it?'

Edward-Jones gave Richard a glowering look. 'If you go on like this, they'll have to take you away in a van. Anyway, what the bloody hell do you mean?'

'Your son's been shooting his mouth off to a fellow prisoner in Brixton.'

'Oh, God!'

'He says that you'd have disposed of his victim's body if it

179

hadn't been discovered before you had the opportunity. Presumably you'd have got rid of it the same way you got rid of Gertrud Klose's.'

'O.K., you want it, so now you can have it.' His tone was hard and full of spite. 'If Gertrud Klose's bones are ever dug up, they won't find anything to connect me with her death, but they *will* find a cigarette case with the initials L.H.D. on it. Her flesh may have rotted away by now, but not that cigarette case.' He gave Richard an almost pitying look. 'And who knows, the local police might receive an anonymous tip-off telling them where to search? So you see, Richard, for all your cocky talk, you're just an amateur playing in a league for professionals. You wouldn't take my friendly advice, so now you must swallow the nasty truth. It was your father who killed that German girl, not me.'

'You're lying,' Richard said, heatedly. 'Frank Hare said my father never came under suspicion, but that you did.'

'Only because I helped my terrified hut mate. I can see his scared face now when he came back and said the girl had suddenly collapsed and died while he was screwing her in a wood. He was a shivering wreck. If it hadn't been for me, he'd have been court-martialled, cashiered, sent to prison and heaven knows what else. He'd certainly never have become Laurence Deegan, the famous Q.C. Hare and his like may have regarded me as an upstart who hadn't been to the right school, but, at least, I didn't behave like a bloody mouse when it came to trouble. I acted first and talked afterwards.'

Richard licked his lips which had become uncomfortably dry. 'If you buried the girl's body to save my father, why did you take his cigarette case and put it in the grave?'

A cunning look came into Tom Edward-Jones' eyes. 'Because I wasn't going to carry the can, if her body was ever found.' With a faint sneer, he added, 'There are limits to friendship. Burying a body is one thing. Standing up and taking a murder rap for someone else is the act of a bloody fool in my book.'

'I suppose you told my father what had happened to his cigarette case?'

'It seemed fair to let him know,' Edward-Jones said with a small smile.

'And you've held it over him as a threat ever since,' Richard said bleakly.

'Certainly I used to remind him from time to time.' He paused and, with a scornful expression, asked, 'Are you happy that you know the truth at last?'

Richard felt himself trembling as he attempted to sort out his thoughts. If only he could think more clearly, he was sure he'd be able to hit back at the man who had propounded such brutal facts as truth. He was still groping for a challenging retort, when Edward-Jones spoke again.

'Apart from your father's reputation as a leading Q.C., it struck me as poetic justice that he should defend my son for doing exactly what he'd done himself thirty years before. Particularly as he'd been luckier than Terry and never been found out. To date, that is. Your father was also nineteen when he had his romp in the woods, same as my Terry.'

'Why did you really want my father to defend him?' Richard asked with a puzzled frown.

'I've just told you. It seemed the right moment for him to return a favour.'

'Despite the fact he didn't want the case?'

'We can't always be choosy.'

'So you were prepared to blackmail him into taking the brief?'

Tom Edward-Jones gave an impatient shrug. 'You're being melodramatic. Why should any blackmail have been necessary? It was a perfectly straightforward case. There's evidence the girl died of vagal what's the word . . .'

'Vagal inhibition.'

'Right! It means she could have flaked out if a feather had touched her neck. We'll call doctors to prove it. If Terry doesn't get off, it'll be because the police have rigged the case against him.'

'Why should your son say he'd have had a stronger defence if my father had represented him?'

'Bloody Brixton Prison seems to be a police listening post,' Edward-Jones said angrily. 'The answer is because your father was the best lawyer in the game.'

'Or because you believed you could put pressure on him to concoct a false defence?'

'I've told you what Terry's defence is. How can that be fudged? It's based on what doctors will say.'

There was something Richard didn't understand. If that was Terry Edward-Jones' defence (and it was what Stanley had also told him) in what way could his father have been susceptible to pressure? And if he had not been susceptible to pressure, why had he felt compelled to kill himself? It didn't make sense.

Tom Edward-Jones had just said it was a perfectly straightforward case and so it appeared to be. Admittedly, Laurence Deegan might not have volunteered to defend, but there seemed to be no reason why he couldn't have done so without harming his reputation or violating his integrity. In which event, why had he chosen instead to die by his own hand? As Edward-Jones had also pointed out, it wasn't a case which lent itself to a crooked defence. So it appeared that, if his father's death *was* connected with the delivery of the murder brief, there had to be some leverage which still lay concealed. The threat of exposure had been there for nearly thirty years, so what had brought matters to their hideous conclusion? It had to be something more than was involved in presenting Terry Edward-Jones' defence.

Aware that his host was watching him intently, Richard stood up abruptly and walked toward the door. There was nothing more for which to stay. Edward-Jones made no attempt to accompany him and a few seconds later he was in the lift.

He half-expected the burly young security guard to stop him. Instead, he held open the outer door and bade Richard good night, as he locked it firmly behind him.

Away from the oppressive atmosphere of Tom Edward-Jones' flat, he found his mind functioning more clearly. One thing had been apparent, namely that his host was not the same confident person he had met at the Croesus Club. He had looked tired and had shown signs of nervousness that had not been there on the previous occasion.

So what? Richard reflected unhappily as he walked down Park Lane.

He reasoned grimly that what Edward-Jones had told him about his father was almost certainly the truth. Exposure would have been enough to blow his world apart and threat of it had been sufficient to make him take the so-called easy way out, after making as sure as he could that the truth would never come to light. For a brief moment, Richard felt like crying aloud in anguish.

But if he had now learnt the truth, it was still not the whole truth. That fact stood out like a sharp spike.

CHAPTER XXV

The inquest was held two weeks later, just after Fay Deegan's return from Torquay.

Since his visit to Tom Edward-Jones, Richard had done nothing further. He had felt like someone recovering from a bad bout of influenza, listless and depressed. A condition which was not improved by the constant reminder that it was self-induced.

There were times when he felt that ignorance would have been preferable: others when he rebuked himself for such craven thinking.

He had told nobody, not even Sophie, what Tom Edward-Jones had thrown in his face. He had simply said that the visit had failed to produce anything further, though she guessed otherwise from his subsequent air of preoccupation.

On the day of the inquest, Richard picked up his mother in a taxi and they drove together to the court. Norris, entirely in black apart from his shirt, met them at the entrance.

The acting coroner was a small, bald-headed man who despatched business with benign efficiency. As he took his seat, he nodded to the two lawyers who were sitting at opposite ends of the row in front of him. One represented the family, at the insistence of Norris who had persuaded his mother it was desirable to have their interests protected. The other had sought a private word in advance with the coroner to inform him that he held a watching brief on behalf of the Ministry of Defence, but hoped this need not be mentioned in open court.

The coroner, who liked to please everyone when he properly could, had agreed without so much as a surprised flicker. He was used to outside interests being represented at the inquests he conducted and seldom asked embarrassing questions in court, provided he had been forewarned.

The only witnesses to be called were Fay, Stanley, the police inspector who answered the call to go to Chambers and the pathologist. The coroner made it clear that he could have summoned others, but that having read all the statements, he considered it unnecessary. He questioned Fay briskly, but sympathetically, and Stanley at rather greater length.

At the end he expressed his condolences to the relatives and said that though the deceased had left no note to explain his action it was quite clear that he had taken his own life with intent and determination. In the circumstances, the least said the better and it remained only for him to record a verdict of suicide. There was no evidence, he added, to indicate what Mr Deegan's state of mind had been and it would not, therefore, be appropriate to add any rider suggesting that its balance had been disturbed at the time.

As they trooped out of court, Stanley approached Richard.

'If you can spare a moment, I'd like to have a word with you,' he whispered.

'Right. I'll ask Norris to take Mum home.'

Fay said, however, that she didn't need escorting if someone could find her a taxi, which a somewhat grudging Norris undertook to do.

'I'll expect you and Sophie to supper this evening,' she said to Richard as she departed.

'There's a café just round the corner,' Stanley said. 'Why don't we go there?' After they had bought two cups of coffee and had sat down, he went on, 'I'm glad that's over. Thank goodness he's not one of the publicity-seeking coroners. Once he's satisfied about a death, he doesn't waste any time. Incidentally, I suppose you know who that other lawyer was.'

'No. I wondered.'

'He had a watching brief on behalf of the Ministry of Defence, but nobody was meant to know. I found out from the coroner's officer.'

'I guessed it might be.'

'That's what I wanted to talk to you about, Richard. I had a visit from that chap who called on your mother.'

'Bernard Powell?'

'Yes. Did you ever discover how he knew about your enquiries?'

'No, but I suspect that Norris tipped off the powers that be. After he had failed to dissuade me himself to drop them, I think he let fall an anonymous word which found its eventual way to Powell's outfit.'

Stanley frowned. 'Why should he have turned to the security service?'

'He believes that Dad was caught up in some extreme political organisation.'

'The Brotherhood of Racial Purity?'

'So you know about it, too!' Richard said in a startled voice.

'I only found out after Powell had been to see me. He produced some cock and bull story about a highly secret document that had found its way into the Kulka brief by mistake and which your father had extracted at his, Powell's request after a phone call. And could he, if you please, search through Mr Deegan's personal papers to find it? I told him he couldn't unless he obtained permission from the executors and he went off in high dudgeon. Needless to say, I took the opportunity of making my own search after everyone had left Chambers that evening. I was determined to discover, if I could, just what Powell had been hoping to find.' He gave Richard a look of triumph. 'And I did. That's what I wanted to tell you about.' He took a sip of coffee and pulled a face. 'Brewed from tree bark!' he remarked, while Richard waited expectantly. Pushing his cup away from him, he went on, 'I found a small black notebook full of jottings in your father's writing. There were telephone numbers and dates, usually with times written beside them. There were also various initial letters including B.R.P. which cropped up several times.'

'Standing for Brotherhood of Racial Purity,' Richard interjected.

Stanley nodded. 'Tucked at the back of the notebook was a duplicated sheet headed Brotherhood of Racial Purity. It concerned a meeting at an address in Chiswick. There were also two

186

names under the heading Czech Embassy and a date last summer. Also quite a few references to B.P.'

'Bernard Powell.'

'That'd be my guess. Once there was an extension number beside his initials, which made me deduce it was different from the one previously used. Your father had memorised the old one, but had needed to make a note of the fresh number.'

Richard nodded keenly. 'What do you think it all added up to, Stanley?'

'My conclusion is, Richard, that your father had so much truck with Powell's outfit that he must have been one of their busiest part-timers.'

'You mean he worked for them?'

'Like many another public-spirited citizen! I couldn't help noticing that the references to the Brotherhood of Racial Purity began soon after he had defended one of their inner circle members. Presumably, Powell saw the chance of persuading him to join on the pretext that he found himself in secret sympathy with their cause as a result of learning about their aims.' He exhaled deeply. 'None of which, I'm afraid, does anything to solve the mystery of his death, Richard. Have your own enquiries got you any further?'

'They're completely bogged down,' Richard said, discouragingly.

Stanley looked thoughtful. 'Perhaps it's as well. With the inquest concluded, we can regard the whole tragic chapter as closed. We shall probably never know why he did it. It can only have been a sudden brainstorm. There really is no other explanation.'

Richard gave a small nod, but made no comment. 'Where did you find the notebook?' he asked.

'It was in a hollowed out dictionary he kept in a locked drawer of his desk. There were a couple of other reference books with it. He used to complain that they were always being taken from his room and not returned, so he decided to keep them locked away in a drawer.'

'Clever of him! What have you done with it?'

'I took it home and burnt it that same evening,' Stanley said with a note of defiance. 'Moreover, you're the only person I shall have ever told of its existence.' After a brief pause, he added, 'I don't mind your mentioning it to Sir Sam if you want. But nobody else, I beg you.'

Richard had not been in touch with Mr Justice Hensley for over three weeks, partly because the judge had been out of London. But he was now sitting again at the Law Courts and Richard decided to call on him and present him with the final fruits of his investigation. The urge to talk to someone was very great and Uncle Sam was the obvious person. Let him share the burden of his knowledge!

Having taken the day off from work to attend the inquest, he had a free afternoon. After parting from Stanley, he phoned the judge's clerk, who told him to come along at four o'clock as Mr Justice Hensley would be working on a judgement in his room all the afternoon until he left for a committee meeting at half past five.

'How did the inquest go?' Mr Justice Hensley asked, when Richard arrived in his room on the dot of four. He listened while Richard described the proceedings, then remarked, 'So the coroner didn't try and probe the background?'

'No.'

'Good! Though I'm not sure I shouldn't have, if I'd been in his position. But perhaps not.'

Richard went on to relate Stanley's discovery of the small, black notebook and Bernard Powell's visit to Chambers which precipitated it. Mr Justice Hensley let out a satisfied grunt as Richard finished.

'I'm glad that part of the mystery has been explained,' he said. 'I imagine more lawyers have been drawn into assisting the intelligence services than any other outsiders. During the last war, of course, you tripped over them in every secret corridor. So where does this leave you, Richard?'

'That's what I've come to talk to you about, Uncle Sam. I need your advice.'

For the next twenty minutes, Richard described his visit to Frank Hare, followed by that to Tom Edward-Jones.

'I've had a couple of weeks to think things over, Uncle Sam, and I'm still forced to believe that what Edward-Jones told me

188

was near enough the truth. That Dad did accidentally kill this girl and that Tom Edward-Jones buried her body, making sure that, if it was ever dug up, everything would point to Dad.'

'That certainly seems to fit in with what you've learnt about the man. Brash, boastful and self-assured, but not exactly chivalrous. But I'm still unable to see why being briefed to defend his son should have driven your father to suicide. He could have defended him perfectly competently without any violation of professional ethics.'

'Exactly, Uncle Sam. So why did he kill himself?'

'It would seem that you have all the bits to put together and make an answer, save one. One vital piece is missing. It was obviously the threat of exposure that drove him to suicide, but what was he being asked to do that was so unthinkable?' He stared across the room as if pondering a legal conundrum. But when he looked back at Richard, he said, 'I gather you've not told your mother any of this?'

'No.'

'I'm glad.'

'I doubt whether I shall tell anyone, though it's a relief to share the knowledge with you, Uncle Sam.'

'Judges make good confidants,' Mr Justice Hensley said with a smile. 'It's part of their training.' In a reflective tone he went on, 'Your father was always highly sexed, I'd say. He was also attractive to women.'

'I've never heard any suggestion that he was unfaithful to Mum,' Richard said staunchly.

Mr Justice Hensley shot him a quick look, but said nothing. His own suspicions about Richard's birth were something he was going to keep strictly to himself.

'I trust you have no regrets,' he said in a kindly tone. 'Moreover, I don't think you should allow what you've found out to diminish your father's memory. There are few men who don't have something in their past which they hope will never be dug up. Your father's only fault was to panic and lie low. And though great distress must have been caused to the unfortunate girl's parents, you have the consolation of knowing that he never intended to harm her. I'm not seeking to whitewash what he did, merely to put it in perspective. Of course, by behaving as he

189

did, he gave a sizeable hostage to fortune in the shape of Tom Edward-Jones.' He paused and gave Richard a smile of encouragement. 'Don't look so glum! Your father reciprocated the devotion you always showed him and was very proud of you. He would probably have preferred that you shouldn't find out what you have, but maybe, in some unfathomable way, you've redeemed him by doing so.'

With these words ringing in his head, Richard walked away from the Law Courts, feeling happier than he had for two weeks. He was even reconciled to never discovering the elusive fragment of truth that would finally explain the mystery surrounding his father's death.

It was one evening three weeks later as Richard was leaving the Yard when the headline caught his eye.

'Property Tycoon Arrested' it read.

He bought a paper and paused on the pavement to look at it. Staring at him on the front page was a photograph of Tom Edward-Jones, dressed in dinner jacket and positively radiating machismo as he partnered an attractive girl on a dance floor.

'Police today arrested Mr Tom Edward-Jones, the property millionaire, and took him to Marylebone Police Station where he was charged with bribery, perjury in an affidavit and conspiracy to pervert the course of justice. It is understood that two other men will be charged with him, one of them an official in the Department of the Environment and that charges of fraud may also be preferred. The police are searching for both men who, it is thought, may have gone abroad. The charges arise out of property deals in connection with which the ministry official is alleged to have accepted bribes and of an alleged attempt by all three men to pervert the course of justice. Mr Edward-Jones will appear in court tomorrow.'

So that was it! If ever a case bespoke a crooked defence! Each of the charges gave off its own smell of corruption and the pressure would have been on Laurence Deegan to support a dishonest defence. Or else!

As he walked slowly along the pavement, Richard thought he could see how the final pieces of the puzzle fitted together. He now recalled that Sergeant Angelo had mentioned a fraud squad enquiry when they had first spoken on the telephone.

Tom Edward-Jones must have been in touch with his father about the impending proceedings, which he would have known about long before his actual arrest. His father would have demurred at representing him and threats, veiled or otherwise, would have followed.

But it was the delivery of the brief to defend Terence Edward-Jones with its paragraph in the instructions referring to the determination of Mr Edward-Jones Senior to have Mr Laurence Deegan's services that must have caused his father to realise there could be no escape. That the murder case would be inexorably followed by one in which he would be required to abandon his professional principles and turn crooked lawyer. Either that or face exposure had been his stark choice.

It seemed to Richard that the final truth had a less bitter taste than he had anticipated. There was still nothing sweet about it, but at least he could now see his father's death not as the easy way out, but as the only honourable course of action.